The Promise

Also by Jane Peart
in Large Print:

The American Quilt Series:
  The Pattern
  The Pledge

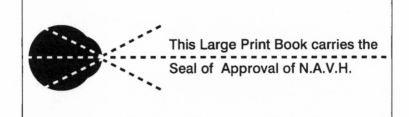

This Large Print Book carries the
Seal of Approval of N.A.V.H.

The American Quilt Series
Book 3

The Promise

Jane Peart

Thorndike Press • Thorndike, Maine

Acknowledgments

The author would like to acknowledge and thank the authors and publishers of the following books, which proved invaluable in the research and writing of *The Promise*.

Joseph Brennan, *The Parker Ranch of Hawaii*

Albertine Loomis, *Grapes of Canaan: Hawaii 1820*

Ruth Eleanor McKee, *The Lord's Anointed*

Margaret G. Martin, Nattie Hammond Lyman, Kathryn Lyman Bond, and Ethel M. Damon, editors, *The Lymans of Hilo*

James Michener, *Hawaii*

Robert Louis Stevenson, *Travels in Hawaii*

A. Grove Day and Carl Stroven, editors, *A Hawaiian Reader*

Armine von Tempski, *Born in Paradise*

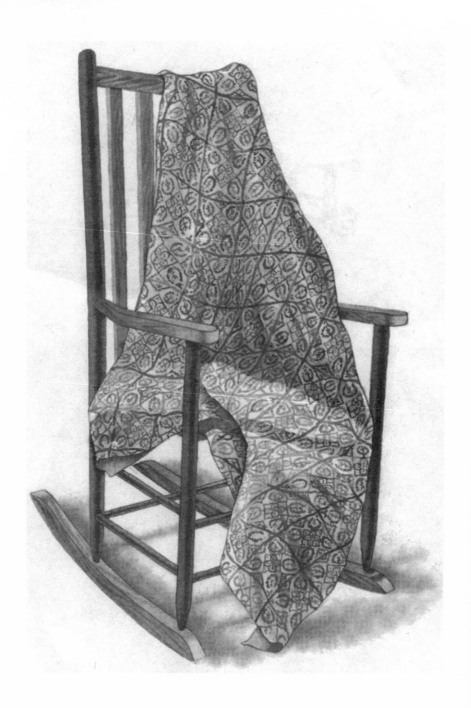

Part 1

Prologue

Jana Rutherford stood looking out from her window at the familiar scene she loved, one she never tired of viewing: beyond the rim of beach, the distant blue line of ocean. As she watched, along the horizon moved a single boat, its sails billowing against the orange-pink sky.

She would never forget her first sight of the Big Island. She had been ten years old and standing at the railing of the steamer coming from Oahu when her father declared, "There it is! Hawaii, the biggest of all the islands."

She had looked in the direction he pointed. The Big Island seemed to emerge out of a sea of turquoise water. Lush green walls of dark tropical vegetation rose steeply above the scalloped beach, onto which the foam-edged surf swirled.

"That's where we're going to live, Jana. That's our new home," he had said. "We're all going to be happy there."

And they had been. Especially Jana. From the beginning, she had loved everything Hawaiian. She even liked her name better in Hawaiian. *Koana.* It sounded softer, more musical, than Jana or Johanna, her christened name.

A gentle wind rustled the fronds of the palm trees surrounding the house and stirred the curtains. Sighing, she reluctantly turned away, back to her bedroom. She still had much to do before tomorrow, when she would leave for Hilo, travel by steamer to Honolulu, and then board the ship that would take her to the United States.

Only one thing left to do, something she had left to the last. This task would seem in some way to tie up the loose ends of her life here in the house where she had lived for the last ten years.

She had to go through the contents of the rectangular koa wood box at the end of her bed. The chest had come with her from Oahu. It held her childhood, and the disposition of all the things stored within would have to be decided upon. It was a job she dreaded and so had procrastinated doing.

Kneeling in front of it, she raised the top. The collection of a lifetime was piled haphazardly within: old dolls long since put away; worn books; toys; a ragged, one-eyed plush bear, too scuffed and limp to be passed along to some other child, yet too beloved to part with; a cardboard portfolio she had fashioned to hold some of the first drawings and watercolors she had done at school; and in one corner, a battered shoe box. When she picked that up, a fine drift of sand spilled over her hands. Inside was an assortment of seashells. Immediately a whole parade of happy days on the beach swept through her mind. It was then that she saw what lay underneath, at the bottom of the chest: her memory book, a little warped, mildewed on the edges, its original pink cover turned brown, the spray of pansies that had been painted diagonally across it, faded.

Taking the book out, Jana sat back on her heels and placed it on her lap. Slowly she opened it and read the first yellowed page.

THIS MEMORY BOOK BELONGS TO
JOHANNA RUTHERFORD

born on Oahu in the Hawaiian Islands, on the occasion of her twelfth birthday, given to her by her loving Grandmother, whose fondest wish is that these pages may only record

sunny hours, noble thoughts, joy-filled days, and happy memories.
                    Johanna Shelby Davison

November 1881

My grandmother, who lives in North Carolina on the mainland, sent me this book. In it I am going to write all the important things that happen in my life. Then when I am old, I can look back and remember what it was like to be a child. Grown-ups seem to forget.

Some important things have happened to me this year. First, I have a baby brother, Nathan. Alani, his nurse (she used to be mine), mostly calls him Nakana or keiki, which means "baby" in Hawaiian. He was such a surprise. When my mother arrived from Honolulu, she was carrying him. He is the most beautiful thing I've ever seen. Like a little doll, with plump rosy cheeks, a little button of a nose, and a tiny round head covered with soft golden hair.

I had another brother, born in California where Mama and Papa lived before they came to the islands. But he died of scarlet fever when he was only a few months old. Mama says he's a little angle in Heaven now. That's why mama was so happy to have me *after* they came to Oahu. And now we have another little boy for our family. Isn't God good?

The second important thing is that we moved to the Big Island. My father, Wesley Rutherford, is now principal of a school in Waimea. My father and I came here first. We came by ship and landed in Hilo, then rode in a wagon over to the home of Mr. Caldwell, the superintendent of island schools, where I am to stay until Mama and the new baby come with all our household things.

The next important thing that happened to me: I met Akela and Kimo. They are cousins. They live with their tutu — that's the Hawaiian name for grandmother. She was in Kohala, at the other end of the island, so they were boarding there, too. I mention this because Akela is now my best friend.

Akela will be in my class when school starts. She is very pretty and very sweet. Kimo is twelve, and two years ahead of us. At first I didn't like him at all. He seemed kind of stuck up. Later I found out they belong to the Kanakui family, known by Hawaiians as the alli. They are considered nobility, because they

13

are descended from the ancient chiefs of the islands. I did not know this until Kimo informed me.

Summer 1882
Akela, Kimo, and I go to the beach to-gether most every day. Kimo likes to be the leader in our games. We climb on the banyan trees, build sand forts, and look for shells in the tide pools. We swim in the shallow water. Kimo has a board on which he paddles out beyond the breakers, then catches a wave and rides it in. He showed me how to do it, too. But I kept falling off. I wish I could go barefoot all the time.

September 1882
Summer is over. I hate for it to end. I love being free of lessons and home-work, and only going to the beach all day. School started today. Edith Preston, the daughter of Colonel Preston of the big Preston Ranch, enrolled this year. She was put in our class, since she is the same age as us. She has been tutored at home until now. Her father wants her to go to regular school and have friends on the island. She has dark eyes but golden blond hair, because she is a hapa-haole.

Her mother was a Hawaiian princess, Akela's tutu told us. Akela and I haven't decided yet if she will be our friend.

September 25th

We've decided to be friends with Edith Preston. Her Hawaiian name is Ekika, which we have shortened to Kiki. That's what we call her. She is fun and friendly. I think we're going to like her, even if she is very rich. We have formed a friendship club: Akela and Edith and me.

October 1882

Kimo is an awful tease. Sometimes I hate him! He does this really maddening thing — he'll pull the ribbon out of my hair and hold it out of my reach while I try to snatch it back. Then he'll recite a terrible singsong: "Johanna, banana, tee-legged, toe-legged, bow-legged Johanna!" I don't know where he got it, but it makes me really angry.

Tutu Kipola says not to pay any attention to him. "He's just trying out being a man." We had so much fun all summer. Kimo went with us most of the time. At school he hardly speaks to us. He stays with the boys. It isn't mana to talk to girls there except to tease.

December 1882

Akela and I went up to the Preston Ranch the day after Christmas. Edith showed us all the things she got for Christmas. I never saw so many presents for one person. Edith's big brother, Bayard, is home for Christmas from the school on the mainland. He never paid any attention to us at all till he heard me call Edith by her Hawaiian name, Kiki. Then he yelled at me. He is so stuck up and bossy. Anyway, we got to ride horses and have fun.

September 1884

I haven't written in here for a long time, because nothing important has happened. This is very important. Kimo is to go to a boarding school in Honolulu, to the Hawaiian Heritage Academy. The fees were provided by a trust fund set up by a wealthy Hawaiian, for pure-blooded Hawaiians only. Akela cannot attend, she told me, because her father was Chinese. Even though I hated Kimo's teasing, I know I shall miss him.

January 1885

Kimo came home for the Christmas holidays. He has grown a lot. At first we were shy with each other, because it seemed he had been gone such a long time. But after a while it was all right. We will always be friends, I think. At least, I hope so.

Summer 1885

I haven't written all summer. I've been too busy. So much has happened. Kimo was back on the island from school. He is helping his uncle in his carpentry shop in Kona during the week, and he's only at Tutu's on the weekends. He graduates from Heritage Academy next year and has applied for an apprenticeship to a famous cabinet-maker in Germany! If he gets it, he will be gone two years!

September 1885

Kimo left for Oahu today. He came to see me last evening to say good-bye. He gave me a beautiful koa wood jewelry box he'd made. He said it was for my birthday, since he won't be here when I turn sixteen. We walked down to the beach together. Kimo wrote in the sand, Kua kau makamaka. *In Hawaiian that means, "Forever friends."*

The rest of the pages of the memory book were blank. Idly Jana turned them. So much had happened since that last entry. And it all seemed so long ago. Nearly four years. . . .

When had she stopped writing in this book? More to the point, why? Could it be because of her grandmother's wish that only "sunny hours, joy-filled days, and happy memories" be recorded here?

Jana sighed and slowly closed the book. She held it for a minute against her breast, then thoughtfully replaced it and closed the koa box lid.

Was it the Christmas of 1885 when everything had changed for her?

Chapter 1

The Big Island of Hawaii
Early December 1885

"I have something so exciting to tell you two!" declared Edith Preston as she, Jana, and Akela left school one afternoon the first week in December. "I've been dying to tell you."

"What is it, Kiki?" Jana asked, using her friend's Hawaiian name. "Do tell. I love secrets."

"Well, it's not exactly a secret, but I had to wait until everything was arranged. Bayard is bringing home some friends for the Christmas holidays. Papa says I am to invite you both to come stay over New Year's. It will be a *real* house party, the kind Papa and Mama used to have in the old days. Papa says he wants to have the house filled with young people, music. There will be a ball and a rodeo. It will be ever so fun."

Jana looked at Edith. Even in her school

19

uniform of shirtwaist and khaki skirt, she was strikingly beautiful. The combination of golden hair, tawny skin, and dark-brown eyes revealed her mixed heritage. Her mother had been a Hawaiian princess, and her father was the owner of the largest ranch on the island.

"So you will come, won't you?" Edith demanded. She halted, her hands on her slim hips, facing her friends.

"I don't know," Jana replied uncertainly. She wasn't at all sure if her parents would allow her to attend such a house party. It might sound too sophisticated.

Bayard Preston, Edith's half brother, was a student at Yale on the mainland. His classmates, the guests he was bringing home, would all be his age, sophisticated college men. Details of Colonel Preston's lavish parties, which were attended by wealthy friends from Honolulu and as far away as San Francisco, fed the gossip mills of Waimea. The Prestons moved in a social world unknown to the conservative Rutherfords.

Although her parents had never done anything to discourage the girls' friendship, Jana's father, Wesley, was the exact opposite of the flamboyant Colonel Preston. She knew that her father disapproved of some of

20

Colonel Preston's projects. His buying up of land and developing it the way he did was one example. Her father often expressed his concern that the very things that seemed to expand the economy also destroyed some of the old ways, the customs of the Hawaiian people. He believed that as more people went to work at the Preston Ranch and other such enterprises, fewer maintained their own small farms and businesses and remained independent.

Her mother's objections would be more personal. She regularly cautioned Jana not to be too impressed by what was taken for granted at the ranch. "Money can't buy happiness, you know." That statement totally bewildered young Jana. Edith, Bayard, and Colonel Preston seemed perfectly happy to her.

These thoughts passed quickly through Jana's mind. Edith looked indignant at her hesitation. She stared at Jana wide-eyed. "Of course you're coming! It's going to be marvelous. Why ever *wouldn't* you come?"

"I'll have to ask," Jana hedged.

By this time, they'd reached the hitching post where Edith, who usually rode to school, tethered her horse, Malakini. As Edith swung herself easily up into the saddle and picked up the reins, she said confidently, "Don't worry. Papa will come and speak to your folks. He can persuade anyone to do anything."

Jana and Akela exchanged a knowing look. Both the other girls were used to their friend's self-assured manner. Rarely did Edith Preston fail to get what she wanted. And no wonder. She had everything: money, position, beauty. Edith rode off, and as they continued walking, Jana asked, "Will you go?"

Akela shook her head. "I don't think so. Our whole family will be celebrating Christmas together in Kona."

Of course, that was to be expected. Immediately the word *ohana* came into Jana's mind. Ohana, the Hawaiian word that symbolized family. A beautiful word, a beautiful reality, which the Kipolas reverenced. But it meant much more. It meant an unbroken circle of relationship that extended beyond the immediate family and included many others. Ohana meant a bond of love that surrounded, protected, the individual so that no one ever needed to feel alone. Jana envied that closeness she'd glimpsed within the ohana. Her own father was an orphan, and her mother's family lived far away in the southern part of the United States.

"But couldn't you even come for a few

days?" Jana persisted. "Over New Year's, like Kiki said?"

"Well —" Akela blushed slightly as she said, "Pelo's family will be there, too."

At the mention of Pelo Kimura, Jana gave her a sharp glance. Were Akela's feelings for Pelo more than friendship? They had known each other from childhood, been playmates. Just as *she* and Kimo, Akela's cousin, were.

They had reached the fork of the road where they turned to go to Akela's grandmother's house. No more was said about the Prestons' house party as they started up the winding hill that led to the home. It stood high on a windswept cliff, overlooking a stretch of white-sand beach and a crescent of blue ocean. Through an arched gate, they passed into a garden lush with color — purple, orange, yellow, pink — and fragrant with the mingled scents of hibiscus, gardenias, and plumeria.

They sat down on the porch steps to take off their high-topped boots, as it was Hawaiian custom to remove one's shoes before entering a home.

Unlacing her shoestrings, Jana asked, "What do you want to do when we finish school, Akela?"

Akela looked startled. "Do? I don't know.

I haven't thought."

"*I* want to be an artist."

"You're very good. Your paintings of flowers and all."

"I want to do more than just pretty pictures. I mean *really* paint. My parents want me to go to teachers college in California. They want me to start sending out applications." Jana made a face. "Ugh! I don't want to teach! All I really want to do is stay right here and have my own little studio where I can see the sky and the sea, and paint!"

Akela smiled. "That sounds nice."

"So when we *are* finished with school," Jana persisted, "deep down, what do *you* want to do?"

Akela's expression became dreamy. "I suppose — something like you — stay on the island, be happy."

Just then they heard Akela's grandmother's voice calling, "Is that you, girls? Come in, I've poured some guava juice, and there are fresh cookies."

"Coming, Tutu!" Akela called back.

Any further discussion of the future interrupted, they pulled off their stockings, ran up the steps and into the house. Mrs. Kipola, tall and silver haired, stood at the door waiting, holding herself like a duchess.

Pekila Kipola's regal bearing came rightfully. The Kipolas were descendants of an ancient clan of royalty called the *alli*.

Inside it was dim and cool. The girls settled down on the floor on straw mats to sip their juice and munch on crisp macadamia nut cookies while Tutu, seated nearby on a fan-backed rattan chair, picked up one of the quilts on which she was working.

Jana glanced at Tutu, then over at Akela. Hawaiian women were all so beautiful — velvety eyed, satin skinned. Kipola had an unusual face, but one of rare beauty. Her full lips seemed lifted in a perpetual smile. Her nose was strong, the nostrils slightly flared, and her dark eyes shone with an inner light. Akela's beauty was more delicate. Her dark, wavy hair framed a perfect oval face. Her hands were slender, graceful. Beside Akela, Jana was always aware of her own *haole* appearance. She took after her father, having sandy brown hair, hazel eyes, skin inclined to freckle.

"So how was school today?" Tutu asked in her low, melodic voice.

"History!" both answered in unison. Then Akela said, "We're learning about the Civil War and President Lincoln." She looked over at Jana. "Tell Tutu what you told me about your mother and father being at the theater the night Mr. Lincoln was shot, Jana."

Tutu looked up from her quilt, shock replacing her usually serene expression. "How dreadful."

"Yes, it was terrible," Jana nodded. "Mama has a quilt she made — not like the ones you make, Tutu, but one they call a memory quilt or crazy quilt. It's made out of all sorts of different materials and fabrics cut from dresses or cloaks that have special meaning in their lives. Mama was wearing a blue velvet dress that night to the theater. And after the shooting and President Lincoln's death, she vowed she would never wear that dress again. So she cut it into scraps and pieced them together for a quilt. She bound the whole thing with black satin ribbon from the bonnet ribbons she wore to his funeral." Jana paused. "It was all very sad."

"It sounds like a sad quilt, a sad memory to keep," Tutu said mildly.

"Well, it's not *all* sad. The whole quilt, I mean. She also has pieces of her wedding dress in it, and the cloak she wore when she traveled through enemy lines with my father when they were eloping."

"Eloping?" echoed Akela, looking puzzled.

26

"Yes, isn't that romantic? They had to run away to get married, because Mama's family didn't approve."

"Oh, now *that* is sad," murmured Akela. "To be married without your family! How awful."

Jana looked from one to the other. She saw at once they did not think it romantic at all, but tragic. To be married without your family, your ohana, was truly a tragedy. The bonds of the Hawaiian family were very strong.

They went on to talk of other things, until at length Jana got to her feet reluctantly, saying, "I'd better be going."

"Will you stay and eat with us, Koana?" Tutu asked, using Jana's Hawaiian name. "Uncle Kelo's coming, and there'll be plenty of 'tell story,' " she promised with a throaty chuckle.

"*Mahalo*, Tutu, thank you. I wish I could, but Mama's going to her mission circle this evening, and Papa is over in Kohala at a school board meeting, so I have to be there with Nathan."

Jana's regrets were sincere. She liked nothing better than to be in the midst of the Kipola family. Even an ordinary time there was like a party to her. There was always such relaxed congeniality and laughter, and

Tutu's brother was an excellent storyteller. He held them all spellbound with his tales and legends of old Hawaii. He liked best to tell stories about the *menehuenes,* the mysterious "little people" of the islands. They were the Hawaiian equivalent of the brownies, elves, or Irish leprechauns.

After Jana said good-bye, she walked down the hill and along the road past the school, deep in thought.

She was truly sorry to miss what promised to be an entertaining evening. She loved the feeling of being accepted as one of them as she dipped *poi,* the starchy mixture of mashed taro that Hawaiians are weaned to and most *wahines* can't tolerate. The first time she had taken a meal at Tutu's, she hadn't liked it, either. But with Kimo's eyes challenging her, she had defiantly stuck her finger into the calabash, twirled it, and taken a mouthful. Truthfully, she had hardly been able to swallow it, but she had refused to give Kimo a chance to make scornful fun of her. Nowadays she managed to take one or two fingersful just to feel part of the family.

The Kipolas represented what to Jana was truly the best of Hawaii: the *aloha* spirit. She had heard that term used so often by her father that one day she had asked Tutu what it meant.

"What is the aloha spirit? Well, little one, I can only give you my interpretation. The first *a* stands for *akaha'i,* meaning kindness expressed with tenderness. The *l* stands for *lokai,* meaning unity expressed with harmony. The *o* stands for *olu'olu,* meaning agreeableness expressed with pleasantness. The *h* stands for *ha'aha'a,* meaning humility expressed with modesty. The last *a* stands for *ahounu'i,* meaning patience expressed with perseverance. This is the philosophy passed down to me from my ancestors."

Jana understood Tutu's explanation, for it was what she herself found most appealing about the Hawaiians she knew: their warmth, charm, and sincerity.

Why had she hesitated to question Akela about Pelo? For all their closeness, there was a reticence about Akela, an invisible line over which Jana had never crossed.

Jana's friendship with Edith was entirely different. They'd had frequent "falling outs." Both were strong-willed individuals, which led to arguments. They had times when they weren't speaking. Jana found her uncomplicated relationship with Akela much easier. Edith, used to having her own way, tended to be bossy, which Jana refused to tolerate. Edith was independent, impatient, restless — but she was also generous, kindhearted, high-spirited, and fun loving, with an adventurous streak that matched Jana's own. When they were in one of their "spats," Jana found she missed her, so their fights usually did not last long.

One thing they quarreled over was when Edith brought up her royal heritage, haughtily reminding Jana that *her* mother was a Hawaiian princess. Edith would declare that her mother's heritage made her more Hawaiian than Jana. In turn, Jana would furiously argue that *she* had been born on Oahu, while Edith's mother had gone to San Francisco for *her* birth. That made Jana the more Hawaiian of the two. This argument usually ended in a stalemate, with neither girl giving an inch. A few days might pass before they would make up and the old argument would be forgotten.

As they grew up, Jana realized that some of Edith's snobbishness was Colonel Preston's fault. From a prestigious eastern family, the Colonel had come to the island as a young man and made his fortune in cattle ranching, a new enterprise on the island. He had built his hilltop mansion, married an American heiress, and had a son, Bayard. Widowed a few years later, Preston had remarried. She was Edith's mother,

30

who had tragically died two years later.

Edith was the adored, cherished child of this brief, blissful second marriage. Surrounded by luxury, Edith had grown up without discipline, lavished with love. Once Jana accepted that Edith's behavior was not entirely her fault, she overlooked the flaws and loved her wholeheartedly.

Kiki, as she preferred to be called, was so much fun, and going to the ranch such a treat, that it was hardly worth it to stay angry at her long. At the ranch, Jana got to ride, and enjoy the life lived by the Prestons. They were allowed almost unrestricted freedom by Colonel Preston. Wearing wide-brimmed sombreros and split skirts, they rode along with the *paniolos*, Preston's hired cowboys, and watched them herd cattle. These men were colorful characters, with their multistriped ponchos and their boots with jangling spurs. They adored Edith, treating her with a combination of courtesy, respect, and loving indulgence. They showed the girls rope tricks, tried to teach them to lasso and how to cut and herd the cattle.

Yes, Edith Preston's friendship was one Jana valued in spite of their differences.

Within a few days, Edith's prediction proved right. Colonel Preston — big, handsome, jovial, attired in a white linen riding coat, polished boots, and a wide-brimmed Panama plantation hat — cantered up to the Rutherfords' house. Dismounting from his sleek white mare, he marched up the porch steps, carrying an armload of gifts — a bouquet of the spectacular red-gold bird-of-paradise flowers, a basket of fruit from his orchards, bags of macadamia nuts. He then proceeded to charm Jana's mother. His gallantry reminded her of her southern male relatives as she recalled her own North Carolinian background. It took only a half hour's visit to win her approval for Jana to attend the house party. So it was settled that Jana would come up to the Preston Ranch after Christmas to stay over New Year's.

Chapter 2

The Wednesday before Christmas, Jana took her Sunday school class — children ages five and six who had learned carols in both Hawaiian and English to sing at the midweek evening service — into the small red frame church.

They filed up crooked steps into the little choir loft. Stationed there, she could oversee her charges as well as lead the singing. She also had a view down into the sanctuary.

They had been practicing for weeks, and now the children's clear voices rose sweetly. "O come all ye faithful, *E he-le-mai ou-kou-ka,* joyful and triumphant, *po-e ma-nao i-o* . . ." The beloved song was familiar to her in both languages. It had been sung to her in her cradle by her Hawaiian nurse when they lived on Oahu, and her mother had sung it to her in English. Almost as soon as she could speak, she had sung it, too. Listening to it now in the church, which had been built by some of the earliest missionaries to the island, she sang along with the children.

All at once the words halted in her throat. She saw *him* enter the side door of the church. Kimo!

Akela had told her he was expected home for the holidays, but somehow she hadn't been prepared to see him. Not quite like this. Her heart skipped a beat, and she lost her place in the hymnal. She had not seen him since last summer when he left for his last year at the Heritage Academy in Honolulu.

Memories of their childhood days flashed into her mind: running barefoot along the sandy shore together; swinging on the low limbs of the banyan trees that fronted the missionary compound; eating the bananas and the soft, tangy mangoes and licking the juice from their fingers; building forts and sandcastles and playing pirates at the cove, their own private stretch of the beach. A flood of recollections swept up in her like the rushing tide. Now her childhood playmate was a grown man.

Jana watched his tall figure as Kimo moved into the Kipolas' pew, sat down beside his grandmother, kissed Tutu's cheek. From Jana's viewpoint, his shoulders looked broader. She couldn't seem to stop looking at the back of his head, at how the dark hair grew in waves and clustered at his neck.

It was with a start that she realized the service was over. Quickly she rose with the rest to receive the benediction and join in the closing hymn. The children around her stirred restlessly, eager to be out in the balmy evening. The congregation began its leisurely exit down the aisles of the church, stopping to exchange greetings and hugs with each other. Suddenly Tutu and Kimo seemed to have disappeared in the slow-moving crowd. Jana hurried to the door, shepherding her little group outside. There she had to control her impatience until each child in her charge found a parent. She looked around, frowning. She hoped she hadn't somehow missed the Kipolas. They couldn't have left already, she thought, searching the clusters of people to see if she could spot Tutu's flower-wreathed straw hat. Tall as Kimo's grandmother was, it might be easily seen. But no, there was no sign of her or Kimo. Disappointed, she gave a deep sigh and turned to leave. Just then she heard a teasing voice behind her say, "Johanna, banana —"

She spun around.

There he was. Tall, taller than she remembered. He must have grown at least two inches. His face might have lost its boyish contours, but the mischief was still in his dark eyes, and his grin was just as wide, his square teeth white against his bronze skin. "Kimo! I thought —," she began, then said, "It's been a long time."

"Too long," he said softly. "Aloha, Koana." He put his hands on her shoulders and kissed her on both cheeks. It was the traditional Hawaiian greeting. Jana wondered why it had brought her tinglingly aware of him. Was it the *way* he had said her Hawaiian name that had taken her breath? They stood there in the lavender dusk, looking at each other as if with new eyes.

Jana struggled to regain her sudden loss of composure. "Tutu must be so happy. She's missed you." Her voice didn't sound like her own at all. It was high pitched and shaky.

"I missed her. I missed everything about the island. Every*one*." He paused as if to let the emphasis on the last word register. "We're going to Kona for Christmas, but I'll be back for New Year's. I want to come to pay my respects to your parents. Then we can spend some time together. I have so much to tell you."

Jana was dismayed to find out that Kimo would be gone the entire week. The Prestons' party was ₊planned to start on the twenty-ninth. That meant she wouldn't be at home when Kimo returned from Kona.

"Oh yes, and I . . . The only thing is that —" She broke off.

"What?"

"Well, what day will you come? I mean, be back in Waimea? You see, I may not be —" Jana stumbled, flustered. For some reason, she didn't want to use the Prestons' party as an excuse. But there was no other explanation. "You see, Bayard Preston is coming home for Christmas, and he's bringing some of his friends with him, and . . ." Her words sounded awkward. That wasn't what she wanted to say at all. What she wanted to say was, "Can't you come to see *me* before you go to Kona, or come back sooner?"

But as she was speaking, she saw Kimo's expression change. "In that case . . ." He shrugged with a show of indifference, leaving his thought unspoken. Then, tossing back the lock of silky hair that had fallen forward on his forehead, he said, "Well, it was nice to see you, Jana. Please give your parents my regards."

"Thank you, I will," Jana replied lamely.

Wishing her a merry Christmas and a happy New Year in Hawaiian — *"Mele Kalikamaka* and *hau'oli Makahiki Hou"* — Kimo turned from her.

37

"Mele Kalikamaka, Kimo," she repeated through numb lips. Helplessly she watched him walking away. In desperation, she called after him, "Give Tutu my love."

He looked around, hesitated a second, then nodded, waved his hand, and was swallowed up in the crowd of congenial people still gathered in front of the church.

Slowly Jana walked home. All her happiness at seeing Kimo again drained away, leaving her feeling let down.

The change in him had taken place when she mentioned Bayard Preston's name. Suddenly she wished she weren't going to the Prestons' house party. Now she would miss Kimo when he came to pay his duty call on her parents. She wouldn't be there to walk with him down to the beach or down to the valley of the twin waterfalls. Somehow she had managed to ruin their meeting, the one she had looked forward to all these months.

When she reached home, she let herself in quietly, still feeling subdued by the puzzling encounter with Kimo. As she made her way down the hall to her own bedroom, she passed her little brother's room and paused.

She could hear her mother's voice with its southern accent, talking to Nathan as she got him ready for bed.

"And when I was a little girl, just about your age, on Christmas Eve we would hope and hope for it to snow."

"And did it?" Nathan's eager question came.

"Sometimes, but not often. Even if it didn't snow in town where we lived, we could see it up on the mountains —"

"Like on Mauna Kea?"

"Well yes, sort of like that. Except that for us the mountains weren't away far in the distance but were all around the town, like encircling arms." A tinge of nostalgia now crept into her mother's tone. "But the air was as crisp and cold as you can imagine. So much so that our noses and cheeks would be as red as cherries. Best of all, if it *did* snow, Uncle Myles would get out the sleigh and it would be getting dark and all the stars would come out, twinkling, and we would go skimming along the icy roads over to Holly Grove. . . ."

Holly Grove. The very name seemed to have a certain magic. Jana remembered her mother telling *her* the same Christmas memories when she was Nathan's age.

"The house would be all decorated, with candles in every window and a fire roaring in the fireplace. . . ."

Jana could imagine Nathan's eyes getting

big with wonder by now. He had not the slightest idea what a fireplace was. It was all like a fairy tale to him.

Jana realized, perhaps for the first time, that talking about Christmases back in North Carolina was important to her mother. Jana suspected there was still a longing in her mother's heart for the place she had left long ago, the people she would never see again. The place that was her "heart home," even now that her home was with all of them here in Hawaii.

Jana could sense that her mother longed to see the pine trees and the dogwoods on the distant mountains that surrounded her North Carolina home, longed to enjoy the autumn colors that blazed scarlet, bronze, gold, and longed to hear the soft cadence of southern voices. Now especially, at Christmas time, those yearnings took form and shape in the telling of the stories to her children. That was the reason, Jana thought, that her mother tried to bring to life for them what was still real for her. Her "tell story" was exactly like what Hawaiians did to keep the old times, the traditions, the customs, alive for the next generation.

Jana smiled. Her mother was not that far removed from Tutu or the other Hawaiian mothers.

40

For Jana, Christmas was not the sound of sleigh bells ringing out in the frosty evening air, or snow-clad fields, or frozen ponds on which steel blades made their sharp clink against the ice. It was the brilliant red of anthuriums blooming by the roadside, the clusters of poinsettias growing wild, the whisper of palm fronds in the soft sigh of the wind, the singing of the surf, and the music of the ukulele and guitar strings.

Jana knew she had a "heart home," too. But it would always be Hawaii. She was sure that if she were ever away, she would be soul-sick for the seamless blending of blue sky and sea. In her deepest being, she would never be quite happy away from the Big Island.

Chapter 3

The Rutherfords' Christmas was full of traditions, ones JoBeth had brought to Hawaii from her childhood in North Carolina. Stockings were hung up the night before and magically filled in the morning. The Quaker background of Jana's father precluded too much emphasis on Santa Claus. But her mother's persuasive plea — "After all, Nathan is still only a baby" — had won over his mild objections. So everyone agreed to perpetuate the myth for his sake.

Of course, the religious significance of the day was reverently observed. After the gaiety and laughter of emptying the stockings and exchanging small gifts, the family went to the morning church service.

Entering the sanctuary, Jana looked around hopefully to see if Kimo by some chance had not gone to Kona. But there were other people sitting in the pew usually occupied by the Kipolas. With a resigned sigh, she seated herself and opened her

Bible to Luke 2:1: "And it came to pass in those days that a decree went out from Caesar . . ."

She tried to concentrate on the sermon. The minister drew some parallels between that long-ago event in Bethlehem and life on the island. "Although pictures sometimes portray the scene of a snow-shrouded stable," he said, "in truth the weather in Bethlehem the night Jesus was born was probably more like that of the Big Island." He suggested, "We Hawaiians should feel particularly close to the Savior in this beautiful place so abundantly blessed with God's creation."

Jana responded to that and felt momentarily uplifted by it. However, her mind wandered. How was Kimo spending Christmas? Had he gone to one of the other small frame churches whose twins dotted the whole island? Then, as she joined in the singing of the familiar ancient melodies in Hawaiian — "Hark the herald angels sing, glory to the newborn King, *Ha-mau e na ka-na-ka, mele mai na a-ne-la*" — it struck her that all over the world, in some places at this very same moment, voices were raised in songs of praise. To God, she thought, the world must seem like one gigantic patchwork quilt with all sorts of colors, textures, patterns — but all one as they sing of his glorious birth, of the new birth possible for all those who believe. Jana's heart was all at once full, bursting with happiness, as she sang the chorus: "Joyful all ye nations rise, *Malu no ko la-lo-nei.*"

On the way home, she swung Nathan's hand as they hurried along the road, singing the merry secular holiday song she had taught him — "Jingle Bells" — until they were both breathless and laughing.

The rest of the day was spent quietly and happily. She helped Nathan build with the block set he'd received, helped her mother set out the punch, and decorated cookies for the open house they usually held for friends in the afternoon. But all the time she half hoped that maybe Kimo had come back early from Kona and still might drop by to see her.

By late afternoon she had given up. By evening, after a sleepy Nathan had been put to bed clutching his new toy boat, she kissed her parents good night and, taking the book they had given her, went to her bedroom. However, her eyes merely skimmed the pages, and she found herself reading the same paragraph over and over. Finally she put it aside. It was no use. She kept thinking of Kimo, of that brief encounter, wishing she had it to do again, wishing she hadn't told him about the house party, wishing even that she wasn't going.

No, that was silly. What difference would it make whether she went or stayed home? Kimo had never been a special friend of the Prestons. Why should he feel hurt that he had not been included in the invitation? No, she knew it wasn't that. Had he expected her to just sit around and wait for him to come by? She thought of all the letters she had written him when he was at the academy in Honolulu. From him there had been only a few postcards, pictures of the Iolani Palace, the gardens, a few lines scribbled, nothing personal. What had he thought of some of the things she had enclosed in her letters? The quotations, the bits of poetry, the small sketches or paintings she had done?

But after all, hadn't *he* written on the sand the same words she had written in her letters? Of course, the ocean had washed up on the beach, erasing those words. Had Kimo also wiped them out of his mind, his heart?

Hawaiian men were stubborn, proud, reluctant to express emotions, Tutu had told her. They were afraid to seem weak or womanlike. But there was exquisite expression in the songs they composed or in their beautiful crafts. Jana took out the koa wood box

45

Kimo had made for her, let her fingers move across its smooth surface. Giving it to her had meant something to him *then*. Did it still?

She put it back in her drawer again. Her mouth pressed into a straight line. Well, she wasn't going to let worries about Kimo spoil the rest of the holidays. She was going to the house party at the Prestons' and have a good time, in spite of Kimo.

Chapter 4

Jana could hardly contain her excitement as her father drove their small buggy up the winding driveway hedged with hibiscus and oleander bushes ablaze with blossoms, past groves of coconut palms. Beyond the gates and the arched sign that read "PRESTON RANCH," at the top of the hill stood a sprawling, white frame ranch house. Its architecture was a mixture of traditional Hawaiian plantation and New England–style farmhouse.

Mr. Rutherford had just pulled to a stop in front of the wraparound veranda, when almost immediately one of the Prestons' Chinese menservants came running out of the house. Dressed in a uniform of immaculate white duck coat and trousers, he smilingly greeted them. He took Jana's suitcase and valise and motioned them to precede him up the porch steps while he followed, carrying her bags.

Through the screen door, they saw a large

woman coming down the center hall, seeming even larger because of the ballooning of her *mumu* — the Hawaiian "at home" dress — made of flowing, lavishly flowered pink, yellow, and green material.

Jana recognized her at once as Meipala, the housekeeper. She had been Edith's nurse when she was a baby and a little girl, then had stayed on to run the household.

"Aloha!" the woman called to them as she approached. Meipala was handsome, with polished mahogany skin and a halo of crystal-sparkled silver hair. "Aloha! Welcome, Mr. Rutherford, Jana." She pulled the screen door wide for them to enter. "Come in and have some refreshment," she invited. "The Colonel and Edith are out riding, showing Bayard's friends around the ranch. But they should be back soon."

"Mahalo, thank you, but I cannot stay." Mr. Rutherford made his refusal of the offered hospitality — a Hawaiian ritual — gracious yet firm. "Duties, you know. Please give my kind regards to the Colonel, though, and thank him for having my daughter as his guest."

"Oh, *this* one!" Meipala gave Jana a hug. "*She's* like part of the family."

"Good enough. Then, I'll be on my way. Jana, have a nice time and be a good guest."

"I will, Papa."

"Don't worry, Mr. Rutherford," Meipala told him. "I'll keep my eye on both young ladies. And it's Edith, not Jana, who has to be reminded of manners!"

"I'm glad to hear it." He smiled, then leaned down, kissed Jana's cheek. "Goodbye, dear. Have a good time."

After the Rutherfords' buggy disappeared around the bend of the driveway, Meipala put her arm around Jana's shoulders. "Well, now, *kaikamahine*," she said, using the affectionate word for "girl-child," "I have to tell Cook something, and then I'll be right back and we'll go upstairs and I'll show you which room you're to have."

"I won't be in Edith's room with her?" Jana asked, surprised.

"No, not *this* time. You'll be in one of the guest rooms — that way you two won't stay up and gossip half the night." Meipala pretended to look stern — an impossible feat, since any movement of her generous mouth showed deep dimples. "But it's right next to Edith's room, so you two will manage!" she chuckled. Then she said, "I'll be back *wikiwiki*," and she waddled off to the back of the house.

Left alone in the wide front hall, Jana gazed about her in awe. No matter how

49

many times she visited the ranch, entering the house always seemed like walking into a palace. Overhead was a huge rock-crystal chandelier hanging from the ceiling. It might have looked out of place in most ranch houses, yet here it belonged. The Prestons' house was filled with such contrasts. Chinese rugs on polished floors of native wood, teakwood furniture, and carved screens mingled with ornately carved Victorian chairs and settees upholstered in red flocked damask.

Through open louvered doors, Jana could see into the drawing room that opened onto the lanai. A huge painting framed in heavily sculptured gold took up most of one wall. Edith had once pointed it out to Jana, telling her that at one time it had hung in a French museum. Her father had seen it on one of his trips abroad, wanted it, bought it, and brought it home. Imagine!

Along the other wall were glass shelves displaying artifacts of Old Hawaii. Above a wide, handsome, native stone fireplace, an antique Austrian mirror reflected the rest of the room's splendor. In the center of the room stood a round koa wood table with intricately carved legs, holding a glass bowl of pink, red anthuriums.

The sound of Meipala's heavy tread on

the polished floor signaled the house-keeper's return. "Everything fine in the kitchen. Getting ready for *pa'ina,* dinner party, tonight. Bayard's pals here." She rolled her dark, merry eyes. "Big doin's." She picked up Jana's suitcase and motioned with the other plump hand. "Come along, I'll take you upstairs."

Jana followed with her valise. "Where are Bayard's guests staying?"

"Colonel put 'em out in one of the cottages." There were three guest cottages located under the kukui trees behind the house. They were self-sufficient, complete, small units — consisting of two bedrooms, a sitting room, a bath, and a lanai — where Colonel Preston's guests could stay for months at a time, and often did. "I think Colonel figured that out there, away from the main house, those boys could make much *kulikuli,* high jinks, and not disturb anyone else." Meipala laughed, a deep laugh that shook her whole body, as if she thought that young men having a loud good time was a great joke.

At the top of the stairs, Jana caught up with Meipala and walked alongside her down the long hall. "Here you are," Meipala announced, opening the door into a large, airy room. "I got plenty to do," she told

51

Jana, "but you can settle yourself until Edith gets here, *pono?*"

"Right. Yes, I'll be fine," Jana assured her.

After Meipala hurried off, Jana looked around with delight at the luxurious room she was to occupy. Sheer curtains billowed at the floor-length windows, which opened up to a second-story circling porch overlooking the lawns and gardens. Dominating the room was an enormous bed with turned railings and carved pineapple posts. It was covered with a beautiful Hawaiian quilt, a design of pale green breadfruit leaves appliquéd onto a creamy background.

Compared to her simply furnished room at home, this was ultimate luxury. *I feel like a princess!* Jana thought as she began unpacking her suitcase, hanging up her clothes in the armoire.

She heard Edith before she saw her. There was no mistaking that gay, laughing voice calling her name, the sound of bare feet running down the hall.

"Jana!"

In the next minute, Edith burst into the room. Grabbing Jana by the arms, she whirled her around a couple of times.

"Oh, I'm so glad you could come! We are going to have a glorious time. Just wait till you see. And just wait until you meet Bayard's friends!" Edith stopped breathlessly and looked around her. "Let me see what you've brought!" She dashed over to the armoire, where Jana had just hung up some of her dresses. Edith held out the skirt of one of the dresses. "Oh, your mother is so clever. You are so lucky, Jana. All my things are store-bought. Aunt Ruthie did send me some dresses from San Francisco. I'll show you later."

As if she had suddenly lost interest in clothes, Edith tossed her hat carelessly off, not noticing that it landed on the floor. Then, shaking out her tangle of golden curls, she plopped down on the bed.

"Bayard's friends are incredible, Jana. One is the captain of the debating team, the other of the tennis club, and the other one — oh, I forget, but something interesting. We are going to have such a good time. We shall be included in everything. I made that crystal-clear to Bayard." Her tone turned severe. "He promised. We are *not* to be sent upstairs or pushed out of sight like babies, as we used to be — this time, we are *in* the party!" She laughed gaily. "In fact, we *are* the party. At least until some of Bayard's Honolulu crowd gets here. They've taken practically a whole deck of the steamer from

Oahu. But," she declared, "by the time they get here, we will have them all eating out of our hands! Now all we have to do is plan our strategy."

Amid peals of laughter, Edith outlined for Jana their plan of action. Since she had met the three young men, she gave Jana a brief description of each one. "I've only had a chance to look them over after they first arrived, because of course Bayard was in his usual form. In total control. But they are all attractive. I've already picked out *mine*. Greg Amory." She giggled. "But he'll not have any idea of it. Instead, I shall act indifferent to him and interested in someone else — Tom Markham. Really a quiet, serious type — I can't think why Bayard would be friends with him. Maybe he coaches Bayard on economics or math!" She picked up one of the pillows, bunched it up, flipped over onto her stomach, and hugged it, laughing.

Amazed, Jana looked at her friend. "Where on earth did you learn all this?" she demanded.

"Oh, I've been doing my homework!" Edith reached under the bed and brought out two glossy magazines and held them up so Jana could read the titles — *Metropolitan Ladies*. "These are full of all kinds of articles, from the latest hairstyles to how to use 'complexion enhancements' subtly, to examples of witty dinner table conversation, to the latest dance steps, to rules of flirtation!"

"You mean, they have *rules* for such things?" gasped Jana.

Edith rolled her eyes. "We have been living in kiddieland, Jana. Girls our age on the mainland go to tea dances and evening parties all the time. To *college* proms! Bayard and his friends are *used* to girls who know their way around — not only how to dance but how to flirt and how to tease and talk to men. It's all a sort of game, you see. Not at all like we're used to — but we can *learn*." She flipped open one of the magazines, then handed it to Jana. "Just look at that."

Jana's eyes traveled quickly down the page, which was headed "Be Interested in Whatever He Is Interested in." She threw the magazine back at Edith. "That sounds stupid to me. Dishonest! Why should we pretend, like this is some kind of childish game of make-believe? Surely you don't believe all this drivel?"

Edith looked indignant. "Well, it's worth a try! I don't intend to be ignored, as we usually are when Bayard is here." Flinging back her hair, she lifted her chin defiantly, her eyes flashing. "*You* can suit yourself, but

I'm sure going to try it." Edith shrugged. "And *tonight*."

Jana shook her head. "I don't think I can change that much. Be any way but just me."

"I don't mean *change*, Jana. I just don't want to be treated like a child anymore. Not by Bayard and not by his friends. *You* can do what you want."

Jana stared at Edith with a mixture of dismay and admiration. Edith was so pretty, so confident. She seemed charged with joyous energy at the prospect of waging a campaign to capture one of her brother's classmates. For her it *was* a game.

Suddenly Jana realized it was a game that she had no idea how to play.

Chapter 5

That evening Jana was dressed first. She was waiting at the top of the stairway, ready to go down to dinner, when Edith came flying out into the hall. Her hair, swept up in a new style, had not been secured properly, and hairpins went scattering in her wake.

"Uh-oh! I'd better go back and fix it!" she exclaimed and went running back to her room.

Jana, who was wearing her hair in the usual way — tied back with a bow — smiled resignedly. There was no use complaining. Kiki was determined to present a grown-up image tonight. And that evidently meant pinning her hair up, however inexpertly.

Jana wandered over to examine the life-size portrait of Edith's mother that hung in the alcove of the landing. Jana had seen many photographs of her. They were all over the house. She had never really studied this gold-framed painting. In it, Ketura Preston, although she was dressed in a gown designed by a famous Parisian clothier and was holding an ostrich-plume fan in one graceful hand, looked every inch the Hawaiian princess she had been.

Looking at it closely, Jana decided that Edith looked more like her mother than she had realized. Except for their coloring. Edith was blond, while Ketura's hair was a gleaming black. However, their features were very much alike. Both had a small, delicate nose, dark eyes, a full, curved mouth. Gazing at the portrait, Jana felt a twinge of pity for her friend growing up without a mother. No wonder Edith was the way she was sometimes.

"All right, I'm ready now. How does it look?" Edith put a tentative hand to the French twist she had managed to achieve, if imperfectly. "Do I look at least eighteen? Twenty?" she asked hopefully.

"You look lovely!" Jana laughed and tucked her hand into her friend's arm and pulled her toward the stairway. "You'll be the star of the evening."

Jana didn't realize how true her teasing prediction would prove to be.

Reaching the last step, they heard the murmur of male voices coming from the lanai, through the drawing room doors. Outside, a purple dusk was just falling. Tiki torches on the lawn illuminated the lanai, where Bayard and his guests were gathered with Colonel Preston. Edith dropped one eyelid in a conspiratorial wink. "Come on, let's make our grand entrance."

"Wait, Kiki," Jana protested mildly, feeling suddenly shy about meeting all these strangers. But it was no use. Edith pulled her relentlessly forward.

"Good evening, gentlemen," Edith announced gaily.

Three white-linen-jacketed backs were to the doorway, and Colonel Preston and Bayard were facing it. At Edith's voice, all three turned with eager smiles. Colonel Preston's face was immediately wreathed in an indulgent smile of welcome.

"My daughter, Edith, and her friend Jana Rutherford, gentlemen," he announced. "Welcome, ladies."

Jana caught Bayard's surprised and rather disapproving expression. Why? she wondered. Didn't he like to see his little sister in her new grown-up appearance? That first impression of Bayard's reaction to their entrance lingered. Did his disapproval include her as well? Was he annoyed that the two girls he remembered as children were being admitted to the grown-ups' party?

She recalled the first time she had seen

Bayard Preston. She had been an eleven-year-old girl, he a seventeen-year-old prep-school boy home for the summer. To Jana, in a way, he had always seemed like a royal prince out of the pages of a fairy tale. Tall, athletic, he had the same tawny gold hair that Edith had inherited from their father. Bayard's manner had been a combination of arrogance and condescension, all characteristics she attributed to royalty.

Even though he had treated Edith and her friends with lofty indifference, it was no more than the young Jana expected of a prince. The Preston Ranch was like a kingdom, with its own rules, activities, behavior. Although Bayard had mostly ignored her, Jana had observed *him*. He seemed as at ease among his father's friends as he was among the *paniolos*. He could ride with the best of them and was fearless in the saddle.

All three of Bayard's guests were tall, well built, nice looking. They did, however, look pale. Of course, they would be, having come from the mainland, where it was midwinter. They were introduced to her as Joel Matthews, Tom Markham, Greg Amory. Then Edith said to Bayard, "You remember Jana Rutherford, don't you, Bayard?"

Bayard lifted an eyebrow. "Not looking

60

like *this*." He moved forward and took Jana's hand, his eyes amused. "Not all grown up. When did this happen?"

"It's a natural process, I'm told," she replied, not meaning to sound clever or flippant. But everyone laughed, including Bayard.

His steady gaze made her feel uncomfortable. She turned away from him to address Joel Matthews, whose boyish good looks and nice smile were less threatening and who seemed eager to talk to her.

"How do you like the island so far?" she asked him.

"It's beautiful. I had no idea. It's my first trip to the islands, you see. . . ." This enthusiastic response was all that someone who loved Hawaii as much as Jana could hope for. They immediately fell into conversation, which was interrupted eventually by the mellow sound of the dinner gong being struck.

Joel offered Jana his arm, and they started into the dining room. On the way, she showed him the brass Chinese gong, suspended between teakwood posts, used by one of the servants to signal that dinner was being served.

Ceiling fans whirred over the beautifully set table, making the large dining room refreshingly cool. Each place held gold-rimmed, hand-painted china settings, crystal goblets.

Seated next to Jana, Joel immediately resumed their conversation.

"After Bayard's invitation, I read everything I could find about the Hawaiian Islands, and I must say, it's more than lived up to my imagination. I hope you realize how lucky you are to live here. What a climate, what gorgeous flowers, what colors. My mother is an avid gardener, and she fusses and hovers over her flowers constantly, but her best prize blooms don't compare with what I've seen here. She'd go out of her mind to see what grows wild on this island."

"I guess we're so used to it, we don't realize how it must seem to *malihinis*."

"Malihinis?" Joel looked puzzled.

"Oh, sorry! Malihinis. Tourists, mainlanders. That's Hawaiian."

"So you speak the language, too?"

"Of course. I was born here."

"Good grief. I didn't realize. What I mean to say is, I hadn't thought of people like you — like *us* — actually being *born* here. Being natives, so to speak."

"Bayard was. Didn't you know?"

"Bayard? Well yes, I guess so. Just never thought. I mean, he's so typically a Yaley! I guess with Bayard having gone to prep school in New England and then on to college there, like we all did — Greg, Tom, and me — I never actually thought of *him* as being Hawaiian."

"Of course, his parents were both *haoles*. Mainlanders. Both the Colonel and Bayard's mother are not of Hawaiian ancestry. But Bayard was born right here. Now, *Edith*'s mother, the Colonel's second wife, *was* Hawaiian. From a royal family, actually — the alli, the clans of ancient chieftains who were here before the white men came."

Joel shook his head. "Fascinating."

Suddenly Jana was conscious that Bayard was regarding her intently. Her cheeks grew warm. She wondered if he had overheard her giving Joel the background of the Preston family. And if he had, did he mind? Flustered, she turned back to Joel. However, now Joel was engaged in a conversation with Edith, who was on his other side, and Jana was left momentarily to her own thoughts.

She chanced another quick look at Bayard. Elegantly dressed in a white linen dinner jacket, starched shirt, and black tie, he looked even more handsome than she'd remembered. At the ranch, where she usually saw him, he wore the rough clothes of the paniolos with whom he rode.

She knew he was a daring rider. Once, she and Edith had overheard a tongue-lashing that the Colonel was giving him for some reckless stunt. They had been in the hall outside the library when the sound of the Colonel's voice, raised angrily, reached them.

"What are you trying to do, break your neck — or worse, get yourself killed?" Colonel Preston had shouted. "Don't you know that this ranch, everything, will someday belong to you? That is, if you don't land in a ditch, or down a cliff, with your fool stunts. Listen to me, young man. I don't ever want to hear of you risking yourself so foolishly again, do you understand?"

Edith, startled, had clutched Jana's arm so tightly that it had left marks. Subdued, shaken, they had tiptoed down the hall and run upstairs, not wanting to be caught eavesdropping.

For some reason that incident came back to Jana now. It took Joel's touching her arm and repeating something to bring her back to the present. "Tell me about the language," Joel urged. "It sounds so musical when it's spoken."

"The Hawaiian language has only a dozen

letters. The five English vowels plus *h, k, l, m, n, p,* and *w.* Sound every letter, even in a string of vowels. Usually you put the accent on the next-to-last syllable."

"Amazing," Joel said with honest awe. "We struggle with Latin at college, but none of us speak a second language. I think it's the American arrogance. Even when traveling in Europe, nobody seems to bother to learn the language of the country in which they're traveling. Instead, we rely on phrase books. Actually, it's insulting to the people of that country."

Listening to Joel's comments, she was impressed by such sensitivity in a man so young. How did he happen to be friends with Bayard Preston, who was about as indifferent to others' feelings as anyone she knew? She glanced across the table at Bayard now. He was telling a long, wild tale about some college prank in which he and a friend had been involved, making it sound hilarious rather than relating how humiliating it must have been for the poor student on whom the practical joke had been played. But that was Bayard — only concerned with himself.

As dinner progressed, the room came alive with gaiety. Colonel Preston could be the most gracious of hosts. The conversation was spirited, punctuated with cross-table quips and laughter. Once or twice more Jana caught Bayard's gaze upon her. There was something challenging in it. Like a dare of some kind. She was reminded of Colonel Preston's warning to his son about his irresponsibility. What reckless venture did Bayard have in mind?

It wasn't long until she found out.

After dinner, back in the drawing room, Colonel Preston suggested that Edith play the piano. When she demurred, he insisted. Edith knew better than to argue further. Throwing a resigned glance at Jana, Edith took her place at the grand Steinway. While everyone was finding seats, Bayard came up behind Jana, took her by the arm, and quietly led her out onto the lanai.

"Isn't this rude?" she whispered.

"I've heard Edith play before — dozens of times — and you must have, too," he said. "I've heard her practicing for years, for heaven's sake. Besides, I wanted to talk to you, and Joel has been monopolizing you all evening."

Jana tugged at her arm and he dropped his grip. The lanai was silver swept with moonlight. The fragrance from the gardenia bushes that bordered it sweetened the night air with a heavy, exotic scent.

Bayard drew a long breath. "You forget about all this when you're gone. It's like learning about the island all over again when you come back. Things change and yet this place remains, somehow, strangely the same." He turned toward her. "Except you. *You've* changed. You're all grown up. I can't seem to get over it. How much you've changed."

Jana didn't repeat the retort she'd made to that same remark earlier.

"Sorry, that was quite blunt for me to say. I don't mean to offend you. My only excuse is that I had the same reaction when I saw Edith. You see, she's always been my little sister to me. I've thought of her that way, talked about her that way. It never occurred to me when I brought home my friends that — well, you see what I mean? I find she's become a young lady. Pretty, beautiful even, and too flirtatious for her own good. Certainly attractive to my friends. Did you notice how Tom was drawn like a moth to a flame? And how Edith was enjoying every minute?"

Jana was amused that Bayard seemed genuinely bewildered by his little sister's transformation. She wondered what Bayard would think if he knew this was exactly how Edith had planned it. Of course, she would never betray her friend.

"Not to say that Joel isn't equally taken with *you*," was his next comment.

"Me? Oh, you're mistaken. He's just very interested in learning about Hawaii, so —"

"Don't be naive," Bayard scoffed. "He could find all that out in a travel book. He is getting immense enjoyment out of hearing it from you."

Astonished, she nevertheless couldn't help being a little pleased at this. Especially to have Bayard notice. Still, she had not consciously used any of the "feminine wiles" Edith had been lecturing her on before dinner.

"You have no idea how very attractive you are, do you, Jana?" Bayard asked, looking at her with his head to one side, as if contemplating her. He took a step toward her, put his forefinger under her chin, tipped it up, studied it in the moonlight. "Know what went through my mind when Edith introduced you? I thought, 'Impossible. That skinny, freckle-faced, long-legged tomboy? Turned into this lovely creature?' "

Jana took a step back from him.

"I'm sorry," Bayard apologized. "I didn't mean to —" He halted. "You *are* quite lovely, but thank God, you don't realize it. At least, not yet. Heaven help us when you do."

He moved away, walked to the edge of the lanai, looked out toward the sea. "I forget how beautiful it is here. I go for weeks at a time — forgetting how I feel when the ship moves into the harbor and I see those steep green cliffs, the rim of blue water rolling up on the beaches. My heart twists in my chest." He turned around, almost glared at Jana. "Do you know what I mean? No, of course you don't. You've never been off this island, and neither has Edith."

He spun around suddenly and said abruptly, "Don't mind me, Jana. I'm always like this my first week back on the island." He changed the subject. "So tell me, what are you planning to do when you finish at the island school? Go to the mainland?"

"I want to be an artist. I'd really like to go to some art school, but my parents think — well, they want me to go to teachers college, which is probably the right thing to do."

"Not follow your own heart?" There was an edge of discernible bitterness in Bayard's voice. "Is that wise, little Jana? There's a quote from somewhere — I don't know where exactly — that speaks of the 'long eternity of regret.' Have you thought of that? No, probably not. Don't mind me. I'm probably transferring some of my own frustration to you." He paused. "You don't have a clue as to what I mean, do you?"

Before Jana could comment, the piano music inside stopped abruptly. Edith's impatient voice reached them, saying, "Oh, that's enough, Papa. Our guests' polite patience has been taxed enough with my playing. After all, I'm not a concert artist!"

A few minutes after that, their mingled voices and laughter floating ahead of them, the rest of the group joined them on the lanai.

Later Jana wondered how her strange conversation with Bayard would have gone if they hadn't been interrupted. Part of what Bayard had been saying touched her. She thought she understood, but she did not know how to express that understanding.

After the others joined them on the lanai, Bayard became once again the genial host. Tom borrowed Edith's ukulele, and the fellows regaled them with college songs. To everyone's surprise, it was Edith who made the first move to end the evening. With an exaggerated yawn, she said, "I'm calling it a night. Tomorrow we go on a sunrise ride and picnic at the head of the valley, remember. Knowing Papa, he'll have us up at dawn. Come on, Jana. Let's tear ourselves away from this fine company." Edith grabbed Jana's hand and playfully dragged her toward the house. "Good night, gentlemen. See you all in the morning."

There were murmurs of protest, but finally the good nights were said and the girls left.

The minute they were inside, Edith rushed Jana across the hallway, up the stairway, and down the corridor till they reached their rooms. There she clapped one hand across her mouth and burst into giggles.

"Didn't I tell you it would work?" she demanded. "I believe I've made a conquest in Tom! And Joel is certainly smitten with *you*," she declared. "Oh, this is such fun! I didn't realize how much fun it would be!"

Jana didn't say anything. She was still thinking about her conversation with Bayard, which was far from "fun." In fact, it had been quite disturbing.

Why had he chosen her to confide in, to pour out such deep feelings to? Although his words had touched something deep within her, how could he have known that they would?

Chapter 6

The next morning, when Jana and Edith came down dressed for riding, the sun was just barely tinting pink clouds with gold. Through the open front door, they saw that Colonel Preston was outside, overseeing the loading of the wagon that was to follow them down into the valley, packed with food for their picnic breakfast. Bayard and his friends were out on the lanai, gathered around a table presided over by Meipala, who was pouring glasses of pineapple juice and dispensing fragrant Kona coffee from a silver urn.

Bayard brought a cup over to Jana. "How do you manage to look so fresh at this hour?"

"Spotless conscience," she smiled, taking the cup from him. "Mahalo."

He raised an eyebrow, then said, "Lucky you. Greg maneuvered us into a card game, and we didn't break up until after two A.M."

"No willpower?"

Bayard grinned. "I was winning. Can't pull out then."

Joel came over and joined them. "Your father says that only experienced riders should go down into the valley." He looked at Jana. "Are *you?*"

"Of course she is," Bayard answered for her. "She's an islander, after all."

"I haven't been on a horse much lately," Joel said hesitantly.

"Then, maybe you'd better not," Bayard said with a shrug.

"Colonel Preston's horses are all well trained. If you just sit back in the saddle and hang on, you'll be fine," Jana assured him. She gave Bayard a reproachful look. He shouldn't have been sarcastic to his guest. There wasn't time for any more discussion, because Colonel Preston clapped his hands and declared, "Saddle up, folks. We're ready to ride."

In front of the house, two of the ranch hands had brought up saddled horses, and the Colonel assigned a mount to each of Bayard's friends. Edith swung expertly upon Malakini, and Jana was helped to mount the sweet-tempered mare she usually rode when at the ranch.

Jana knew that Waipi'o Valley was considered by islanders to be one of the unrecognized wonders of the world. It was where the menehuenes were supposed to live, in the deep rain forests. The valley featured great soaring cliffs with waterfalls that fell a thousand feet and glittering lava beaches that looked like acres of black diamonds. Orchids bloomed, and the white-blossomed coffee plants called "Kona snow" grew.

She also knew that the way down on horseback, an almost perpendicular trail to the bottom, was a frightening test of courage, at least the first time. She could not help but wonder if it had been such a good idea to take these mainlanders on such a scary trip. Of course, that was Bayard and Colonel Preston's decision, not hers. She realized that Bayard and Edith had done it often, challenging each other. The competition between brother and sister had always been fierce.

She had not been down into the valley this year. Her schoolwork — including her extra studies in math and science with her father, who was preparing her for college entrance exams next fall — had taken much time. Time she used to spend with Edith at the ranch.

As the group started out in the beautiful morning with its fresh, flower-scented air, Joel fell back to ride alongside her.

"Bayard says this valley is special. Spectacular views, that sort of thing. True?"

"If you've thought Hawaii beautiful thus far, you're going to be really impressed. The valley *is* spectacular."

"I'm sure it has a story," Joel smiled. "Like everything else here."

"Of course," Jana nodded. "It was once called the Valley of the Kings. It is where the great Kamehameha was taken for safety after his birth, to become the great warrior king who defeated all the other chiefs and united the islands into one sovereign state."

The pace picked up, with Edith and Bayard at the head of the group as the riders thundered through the small, sleepy town of Waimea, their horses' hooves pounding the dusty streets. Waimea looked like a transported New England village, with its brightly painted wooden houses decorated with gingerbread on porches and roof peaks. As they rode by, the cool wind held mingled smells of the rich countryside as well as the briny smell of the ocean. On the way to the valley, they passed hillsides of macadamia nut orchards, sugarcane fields. At last they came to the head of the valley.

Even though she had made this trip a number of times, there was always that heart-chilling moment when they reached

75

the top of the torturous path. They would have to go single file down the steep, wooded hillsides stretching down to the valley half a mile below, where a river wound its way between patches of taro, the plant from which poi is made.

First Colonel Preston and Edith started down. Bayard had pulled to one side, letting his guests go next — he would follow, going last. Jana heard him say, "Your turn, Jana. I'll be right behind you."

She held her breath. Her hands tightened on the reins as her horse stepped off the cliff and began the descent. Her heart pounded. Once started, there was no turning back. She always forgot how steep it was, but she never dared look over the sheer drop into the valley. She was conscious of Bayard behind her, saying, "Lean back in your stirrups, Jana." Instinctively she shut her eyes and leaned forward, putting both arms around the horse's neck. Her horse, Palani, was as surefooted as a mountain goat, and before she knew it they were at the bottom. Finally, hearing his hooves splash into water as the group crossed the edge of a narrow stream, she opened her eyes. She had to blink at the glorious scene bursting upon her. The walls of the valley rose majestically. The tops, etched against the pale blue sky, were purple. Jana drew in her breath. It was like a painting on a Japanese screen. There were dark koa trees on the shady side, and yellow-green kukui trees on the other.

Deep down, surrounded by the sheer cliffs, were taro fields. All sorts of fruits and vegetables grew abundantly here as well: passion fruit, guava, and tiny, sweet bananas.

The double waterfalls were most breathtaking. Cascading like a filmy veil over green ferns and rocks, their beauty was otherworldly. From Tutu's brother, Uncle Kelo, Jana had heard the "tell story" represented by their beautiful twin falls. It was the sad yet romantic island legend of two separated lovers. Dismounting, she led her horse over to the stream to drink. Bayard sauntered over to where she and Joel stood.

"Well, was it worth it?" Bayard asked rather sardonically of Joel. However, his eyes were on Jana as he asked the question, and she felt it was her answer he wanted.

"Yes. Well worth the trip," Joel agreed quietly. Jana glanced at him, realized he was almost too moved to speak. Then Bayard strolled away and Joel turned to Jana. "I wish I had longer to stay. There is so much I'd like to explore and discover about Hawaii."

"You must plan to come back."

"Would you be my guide if I did?" he asked. Although it was spoken lightly, Jana had the feeling that there was more meaning in Joel's question. In spite of the fact that she hadn't tried any of the flirtatious suggestions outlined in the magazines Edith read. Could Edith be right? Was Joel "smitten?" Joel was very nice, but —

Wherever her thoughts were going, they were interrupted by the mule wagon rumbling down the path and Edith calling everyone to come eat.

The Prestons' Chinese cook and his helper turned the buckboard into a bounteous buffet table. The riders, their appetites sharpened by their early morning expedition, did justice to the delicious food.

Luscious pineapple spears, crescents of papayas, mangoes, bananas, an assortment of rolls, sweet breads, and creamy mounds of scrambled eggs, sausage, and bacon kept hot in a small hibachi were heaped on plates, and mugs of fragrant, hot coffee were poured.

Edith looked charming in a boy's blue cotton shirt, suede weskit, a wide-brimmed straw hat banded with a wreath of fresh flowers — the Hawaiian touch — her head thrown back, laughing and joyous. She was having the time of her life. How had Kiki learned to be so comfortable among Bayard's sophisticated college friends, to be so adept at banter and flirting, wondered Jana. Those magazines?

Jana walked a little way down the black-sand beach, and in a few minutes she heard footsteps behind her, turned, and saw that Bayard had followed her.

"A penny for your thoughts?" he offered.

"Not worth it. Just enjoying this lovely place. Wishing I had my paint box and sketch book! All this beauty. I'd like to capture it somehow. Correction — *try* to capture it. I'm not nearly good enough, of course. Still, I'd like to."

They walked along together in silence for a while. Then Bayard said, "What did you think of my little outburst last night?"

Jana stopped walking and turned to look at him.

"Just that you were being very honest. About your feelings, I mean."

"I seldom do that — or I should say, get a chance to do that." He paused, glanced at her. "It was an impulse, maybe, but somehow I thought you might understand. Did you?"

"I'm not sure. I've never been off the island, you see. Well, not since I came here from Oahu when I was eleven. So I've never had the kind of experiences you were talking about."

Bayard stooped and gathered some small stones in his hand, then stood and tossed them one by one ahead of them.

"It is different on the mainland," he said. "You can't imagine some of the stupid questions I get. It usually starts when I'm introduced at a party or somewhere. And you know how it goes, those stiff, clichéd openings to conversations. What I hate most is always explaining myself. 'Hawaii? You're from *where — Hawaii?*' I get so sick of hearing that sort of appalled tone in people's voices. Like you're from outer Mongolia. They look you over, almost as if to see whether you're wearing shoes — or a loincloth." He shook his head. "I'm like a man wearing two hats or standing with a foot in each world: the United States, the rockbound New England of New Haven, the bastion of conservatism, where everyone wears a mask to conceal their emotions — then *this*. All this lushness, these soft-spoken, velvet-eyed, kindhearted people, generous, gracious —" He broke off. After a pause he said tightly, "That could be good or bad. It's kind of a homesickness. Island sickness, actually. On the mainland, I think I play a kind of part, all the while having a terrible yearning to be back *here* where I *know* who I am, how I'm supposed to act, what I'm supposed to say and do." He halted. Facing her, Bayard threw out his hands in a kind of hopeless gesture. "Do you understand at all what I'm saying?"

She saw a sort of desperation in Bayard's eyes, a need to be understood, and she instinctively responded to it. "Yes, I think I do."

"Wait up, you two!" a voice behind them called, and Joel came running down the beach to catch up with them.

Bayard muffled a groan. "Oh, no." However, when Joel reached them, Bayard was the affable friend again.

Jana was sorry yet relieved that they had been interrupted. Bayard's sharing left her confused. Why was he choosing *her* to tell his innermost thoughts to? She was moved by his honesty, touched that he trusted her with such intimate revelations. Yet what was she to say or do about it?

But the moment was past. Bayard again was the smooth, slightly mocking young man she had always believed him to be. If he had allowed her a glimpse behind his polished facade, it was over. And there wasn't anything she was supposed to do about it. Instinctively she knew that certainly she was never to bring it up.

Back at the Prestons' that afternoon, the girls bathed and rested while Meipala rubbed them both with kukui oil, kneading their muscles so all the stiffness of the long ride was massaged away. They both fell asleep and didn't awaken until the evening shadows crept into their rooms and they had to hurry to get dressed for dinner.

As Jana had anticipated, Bayard completely ignored her. It was as though the time on the lanai or in the valley had never happened. It stung a little, but Joel and Tom were so flatteringly attentive that Jana was diverted and did not notice when Bayard excused himself and left the party before the others.

Tired from the valley excursion, everyone decided to call it an early evening. The next day would be even more full. Tomorrow was the rodeo and then that night, the New Year's Eve ball. Jana felt somewhat let down as she and Edith went upstairs. But Bayard's behavior should not have surprised her. That was simply Bayard's way. She blamed herself for being so vulnerable.

Chapter 7

A buffet luncheon was to be held before the rodeo, scheduled to start at one o'clock. Colonel Preston's guests from Kona and Hilo began arriving in their carriages at eleven. As each one entered, they were given a *lei* — a garland of flowers, white or pink carnations, plumeria or hibiscus — which was placed around their necks. The women were dressed in pastel-colored ensembles, carried matching parasols, and wore large-brimmed hats to shade their faces from damaging sunlight during the rodeo. These were the ladies who graced the society pages of the local newspapers, and Jana found herself observing them with awe. They looked like some of the fashion models in Edith's magazines. Her own simple cotton frock looked decidedly plain in contrast.

Colonel Preston was in his element, expansive in his favorite role of jovial host. He welcomed his guests, ushering them into the dining room. There was spread a lavish feast served by uniformed servants. Platters of fresh fruits, several kinds of salads, hot dishes of shrimp and *mahi-mahi* — a tender, white fish — steaming platters of rice and baked chicken papaya, as well as some traditional Hawaiian food made for the special occasion and to tempt the guests, such as *kulolo,* a delicious pudding of taro and coconut cream, were laid dout on the fully laden tables before them.

Colonel Preston's voice boomed over the others as he held forth about the rodeo, an annual event on the ranch, bragging about his paniolos. "There'll be some local lads competing, too. But *my* men are the best. I only hire the finest. Good with horses, fearless riders. You're going to see stunts today you'd never see in a rodeo stateside, not even in California or Texas."

Jana caught a skeptical glance pass between Greg and Tom, but Joel said enthusiastically, "I can't wait, sir. Hawaii continues to amaze me. Somehow I never connected it with rodeos. I never imagined a real cowboy Wild West show put on here — in a tropical *paradise!*"

Colonel Preston looked smugly pleased. "You've never seen anything like it. You're in for a *real* treat, I'll tell you."

At this statement, Jana saw Greg Amory suppress a supercilious smile. Immediately she felt a rush of resentment. Of all Bayard's guests, she liked Greg the least. He had a superior attitude that made her feel defensive. What *did* Kiki see in him? Why not pick Joel, who was so open and seemed to love the island, the ranch, and everything?

Just as she was thinking about him, Joel came over to Jana, saying, "Tell me, what's the history of this? I can't help saying that this ranch, the cattle, and the rodeo here in Hawaii has me totally baffled. The rodeo isn't just to show off Colonel Preston's cowboys, is it?"

"It's more than that," Jana explained. "The cattle were brought from California as gifts to King Kamehameha. Before there were any ranches, they ran wild in herds, eating forests, trampling taro patches. So cowboys from Spain and Mexico were brought here to teach natives how to ride, rope, round them up, keep them on fence-bound ranges. From that, the ranching business began here. Now there are several cattle ranches on the island. Colonel Preston's is one of the largest."

"How did the rodeos get started?"

"It seemed to just develop naturally out of the paniolos' competitive spirit. Their rivalry with each other. It became a real challenge to see who could ride and rope the best. They started having different kinds of races and competitions. I guess you'd say it just evolved and became an annual event here at the Preston Ranch. As you can see, people come from all around to see it. There are parties everywhere afterward — and before too, I guess. It's a really special time."

Overhearing Jana's explanation seemed to have caught Greg Amory's interest. Standing nearby, he leaned toward her, asking, "So these Spanish and Mexican cowboys stayed on in Hawaii?"

"Some did, but the Hawaiians they taught their skills to took to it right away. They loved everything about it: the high-horned saddles, long spurs, and braided lassos. It was just the sort of thing that appealed to them. The excitement, the style, the danger, the risk, the daring of the buckaroos. They have their own version of all they have learned," she laughed, "which is even wilder, more reckless, than anything they were originally taught."

"And the name *paniolos?*"

"It's a kind of 'pidgin' translation of the word *Español,* which of course means Spanish, which most of them were, originally."

Greg seemed about to ask something more, when Colonel Preston went to stand in the dining room arch and waved his hands for silence then announced, "All right, folks, we should be on our way. Ladies and gentlemen, your carriages are being brought around. You'll ride down to the far pasture, where the rodeo ring is set up. A grandstand and bleachers will accommodate you there. For you young people, the large ranch wagon will service you. It's a little rough, but it's a short ride. Let's get going. You young people, don't delay. When *I* get there, the rodeo starts."

Evidently Edith had decided to ride her horse and go ahead of the rest with her father. Jana saw her touch Greg's arm, tip her head coquettishly, and whisper in his ear. He laughed and she looked back over her shoulder at him as she went out of the room. So she was now making Greg her open target, Jana mused, hoping her friend hadn't overplayed her hand.

Bayard rounded up his friends, and Jana found herself escorted by both Greg and Joel. The large wooden wagon, with three rows of seats drawn by four of the ranch's dray horses, was waiting for them out front. Greg Amory helped her up into the wagon, then took a seat beside her. Joel sat down on the other side. Bayard threw her an amused glance and sat down across from them with Tom.

Arriving at the high pasture, they saw that the wide corral had been turned into a rodeo ring. The rustic fencing was now festooned with bright banners. Multicolored streamers tied from each fence post blew in the wind.

Most of the bleachers were filled by townspeople who had ridden up from Waimea for the show. Colonel Preston had a box of seats in the front for his guests. Edith met them and immediately linked arms with Greg and Tom, and they took their places in the front row. Joel and Jana followed. Bayard seemed to have disappeared for the moment, and Jana wondered if he had decided to ride after all. She noticed that Edith seemed to be concentrating on Tom. For effect, she was also waving and greeting people she knew who were sitting around them. Was she trying to impress Greg? If so, he didn't seem to be paying much attention to her. In fact, he looked rather bored.

As they settled in, Jana saw groups of men on horseback assembling at the far end of the field. Those were the riders who would be competing. She pointed out some of the events on the program to Greg and Joel — neither of whom had ever been to a rodeo before — explaining what they could expect. She had decided not to be put off by

Greg's aloof attitude. It was a kind of challenge to get him actually interested. The excited expectation that was tangible in the air would be contagious.

"It's really fun," she told him. "You'll find yourself yelling your head off!"

"*Me?*" he protested. "I doubt it."

"Wait and see!"

Colonel Preston, mounted on his handsome white horse, circled the center of the ring, waving his arm and shouting instructions to the rodeo riders lining up at the starting gate. Then he cantered up in front of the bleachers, took off his wide-brimmed, white felt Stetson, and bowed — as did his horse — to a burst of applause and cheers.

"Ladies and gentlemen, our rodeo riders will now promenade so that you can pick your favorites," he announced dramatically. "Then the games will begin!"

Loud applause mixed with "yahoos" greeted this pronouncement. Jana heard Greg Amory murmur to no one in particular, "What a ham!" Jana bristled. Such a rude comment to make about his host, she thought. For all his so-called background, she was beginning to think Greg Amory was a boor. Accepting the Prestons' generous hospitality obligated him to be at least respectful. She gave him a withering glance to let him know that his remark had been over-heard. But he wasn't looking, for at that moment the thundering of dozens of horses' hooves pounded over the dusty ground as the festively attired paniolos galloped into the ring one after the other. The spectators rose, cheering and screaming.

The paniolos wore sombreros of woven palm, leis of fresh flowers, red sashes around their waists, high leather leggings over white duck pants. Braided leather lariats wound in circles hung from their saddles, and spurs jangled from their boots.

As they passed by the grandstand, each horseman slowed his horse, whipped off his hat, bowed in his saddle, and then, touching his mount's foreleg with his sombrero, made the horse also do a semblance of a bow. One gleaming black horse cantering up to take its turn particularly caught Jana's eye. With a flourish, the rider removed his hat and re-vealed what the shadow of the brim had hidden. Jana gasped. It was *Kimo!* Sponta-neously she jumped up, clapping her hands. He breasted his hat, shook back the thick, dark waves from his forehead. His eyes held laughter, his smile was broad. He was en-joying his surprise. Had he planned to be in the rodeo all along? Or was this a last-minute decision? Either way, Kimo was here and would compete with the best the Preston Ranch could offer. Her heart thrummed excitedly. She knew him to be a superb rider. She had seen him on horseback many times. No question — *he* was her favorite paniolo for today's competition. He gave his sombrero a cavalier twirl, then whirled his horse around and was gone in a clatter of hooves, a cloud of dust.

After that the rodeo took on a much more personal interest to her. In every event, she eagerly awaited to see if Kimo was going to participate in it.

One by one the events of cutting, barrel racing, calf roping, and steer throwing were called. Waiting to see if Kimo was entering, she sat on the edge of her seat. She remembered that the Heritage Academy maintained a livestock ranch to partially support itself. Most probably, Kimo had worked there to earn the tuition and fees not included in his scholarship.

The only event in which he didn't compete was the bucking bronco contest. This always brought the audience to its feet, screaming, yelling, and rooting for the daring ones who entered the event. Hardly any survived longer than a few minutes. The crowd shouted and cheered for their favorite, groaned when one "bit the dust."

Buckled on, the riders bounced, flipped, and circled as the horse tried to get the burden off its back and everyone roared encouragement.

Jana was glad Kimo was not entered in this one. She had already gripped her hands into fists as he did the cutting, the relay, and the barrel racing. Her nails bit into her palms, which now were burning and stinging. Her throat was raw, her voice hoarse, from all her shouts.

"You really go in for all this, don't you?" a sarcastic voice beside her asked. She turned and saw Greg Amory's cynical smile.

"Yes, I guess I do. You'd have to be dead and embalmed *not* to!" she retorted. Then she turned around, feeling suddenly foolish. She shouldn't have lost her temper. Greg wasn't worth it. Had she made a spectacle of herself with her show of enthusiasm? No! Everyone else was doing the same thing, shouting, cheering, yelling. It was *Greg* who was out of step. *He* was the one.

It took Joel to really call him on his attitude. "What's wrong with you, Greg? Come on, show a little life. Remember the saying 'When in Rome, do as the Romans do'?"

"I guess so. It just seems — well, I can't believe this is taking place in Hawaii. You'd think it was some one-horse town in Montana or

Wyoming. To think Bayard comes from all this — it seems odd somehow."

"Didn't he tell you he lived on a ranch?" Jana asked coolly.

"Oh, I suppose he did. But it was never — well . . ." Greg shrugged, not finishing whatever he was going to say.

"If you'd ever seen him ride, you wouldn't think it so odd!" she flashed back, wondering why was she defending Bayard against his friend.

Just then Colonel Preston's voice came through the megaphone he was holding. "And now, ladies and gentlemen, the grand finale. Each paniolo will ride by and give his talisman to the lady of his choice."

Jana watched eagerly as the parade of colorfully dressed paniolos in full regalia began. Keeping their horses beautifully in control, the mounted men trotted into the ring. Moving with precision and pacing the high-stepping horses, each approached the grandstand.

One by one they came, waving their hats as the crowd applauded, cheered. In front of the reviewing stand, as a mark of special gallantry, each paniolo halted his mount, bowed, and tipped his hat. Then, unfastening the broad ribbon he wore across his chest, he handed it to his special "fair lady" among the spectators. At each presentation, there was more applause and cheering as each lady rose to receive her talisman. Sometimes a bold paniolo would lean from his saddle and plant a kiss on her cheek.

When Kimo came riding up, Jana's heart almost stopped beating. He drew his horse to a stop in front of her, swept off his sombrero and bowed to her, then held up his yellow satin ribbon with its cluster of ribbons for her. Joel nudged her. "Jana, he means *you*," he prompted. "Go on. He intends for you to accept it."

Hoping that in her excitement she wouldn't stumble, Jana got up and made her way to the edge of the box, held up her hand to receive the honor. Kimo smiled. Using her Hawaiian name, he handed her the talisman. "Aloha, Koana."

"Mahalo," she said huskily.

He tipped his hat, replaced it, then flicked the brim with his hand and rode off while she stared after him.

Her heart was pumping. Her breath caught in her throat. Kimo, her knight in shining armor. It was as if all the old fairy tales, all the romantic legends, all the poetry and music, all the dreams she had ever dreamed, had suddenly come together in this magic moment.

Chapter 8

The New Year's Eve ball was to be a gala event. Edith was wildly excited at the prospect of her first "*really* grown-up party." For Jana the best part of the house party was Kimo's surprise appearance at the rodeo. Whatever she had felt in their meeting outside church before Christmas, all that strangeness had melted in the warmth of his smile as he handed her his trophy. Nothing could match that moment. Jana packed the ribbon carefully into her suitcase to take it home with her. She was already looking forward to when Kimo would come to see her.

New Year's Eve at the Preston Ranch was always widely attended, and talked about for weeks afterward. Detailed descriptions of the music, the food, the gowns, the decorations, and the flowers would usually take up columns in the society section of the local paper.

In the past, Jana and Edith were relegated to the balcony overlooking the entrance hall, and would peer through the koa balustrade, watching the guests arrive. Meipala called it *okolehaeo,* a good-time kind of party. Of course, in the days when Edith's mother was alive, she told the girls, there had been many of those types of parties.

Tonight's affair was special not only because *they* were going to attend it, but because it would also be the send-off for Bayard and his guests. The next day, they would leave on the steamer to Honolulu, then take the ship back to the mainland.

The ball would not begin until ten, but Edith and Jana started their preparations much earlier.

When she had returned from the rodeo late that afternoon, Jana took out the party dress her mother had made, examining it critically. It was one of the prettiest and fanciest she had ever owned, a blue voile with faceted lace seams, a bowed sash, and a ruffled skirt. At home it had looked fine, but here it somehow didn't look right. After observing the elegant gowns the other guests had worn to the rodeo, Jana could only imagine what their ball gowns would be like.

She knew that Edith's Aunt Ruthie in San Francisco had sent her a dress from some exclusive shop there. Jana felt guilty finding fault with something her mother had spent hours making. Yet it just wasn't right for a grand ball.

Well, there was nothing to be done about it. She would have to make the best of it.

Just then she heard Edith call her. "Jana, come here for a minute, please. I want to show you what I'm going to wear."

Trying to hide her dissatisfaction about her own dress, Jana called back, "Coming."

When she walked into the adjoining bedroom, to her complete surprise she saw Edith standing in front of the full-length mirror wearing a turquoise blue *holoku*, a long, one-piece gown styled after the type the missionaries had first made for the native women, but now fitted, with a yoke and a train.

"What do you think?" Edith half turned for her friend's reaction.

"It's gorgeous! But where did you get it? Surely that's not what your aunt sent from the mainland, is it?"

"No, it belonged to my mother! Meipala has kept all Mama's Hawaiian dresses. It fits me perfectly. And I'm going to wear it tonight!"

Jana had never seen her friend look so lovely. "Oh Kiki, you look beautiful!" The dress itself was breathtaking. The color perfectly set off her apricot tan skin, her dark, shining eyes, and her golden hair.

Still viewing herself critically in the mirror, Edith pointed to two gowns spread on top of the quilt on her bed. One was a scarlet velvet, the other a blue green silk. Jana tentatively touched the material. It felt luscious.

"Those are the gowns my aunt sent. But I've decided to be my Hawaiian self tonight. Why don't you wear one of them? Either one should fit."

"Oh Kiki, I couldn't. Not possibly. Your aunt meant them for you —"

"Of course you can. Go ahead, pick the one you like best!" ordered Edith. "You *are* going to wear it."

Jana stared at her friend incredulously. She shook her head.

"You *must*, Jana. Think of it as a dress-up occasion. Playing pretend, the way we used to. Going to our first ball. It will be only this once. The *blue* would be perfect for you. Do take it and try it on, Jana!" Edith gathered it up and thrust it at her. "Here!" She took Jana by the shoulders, turned her toward the full-length mirror.

Jana held the dress up to herself and looked at her reflection.

"See for yourself! It could have been made for you," Edith declared triumphantly.

Jana *did* see. It *was* very becoming.

"There are slippers to match." Edith brought out a shoe box. "And I know we wear the same size." She rustled back tissue paper and brought out narrow blue satin pumps with French heels and rhinestone-sprinkled bows. She held them out for Jana to admire. "Now, I won't take no for an answer. You *must,* Jana."

Jana had come up against Edith's indomitable will before. Once Edith had made up her mind about something, it was useless to protest. This time Jana didn't really want to. She had never wanted anything so much in her life as to wear this beautiful dress. "Well," she said slowly, "if you *insist.*"

"I *do!* So it's settled. Go ahead, put it on," Edith commanded.

Back in her room, Jana placed her own dress back into the armoire with a brief pang of guilt. But, she told herself, this *was* after all a very special occasion. She felt like Cinderella, whose fairy godmother had provided her with an undreamed-of chance to go to the ball in a beautiful gown. Besides, her mother would never know.

Meipala came to see them before they went downstairs. Her dark eyes misted as she regarded Edith. "So like your mama," she murmured. She had brought a wreath of fresh flowers that Edith wanted to wear on her hair, which she had brushed out to hang in shimmering waves to her waist.

Jana needed some help with the fasteners and tiny buttons on her borrowed dress, a designer creation. She had never seen a dress constructed such as this. Lined in satin, the skirt was gathered to the back in a modified bustle falling into graceful folds. The bodice was separate, tapering to a point at the waist. There were huge, puffed sleeves and a portrait neckline. The blue dress deepened the color of Jana's eyes. Edith was right: the dress could have been made for *her.*

At last it was time to go downstairs.

The lower part of the house had been transformed into a fairyland of flowers and light. Ferns were everywhere — giant tree ferns stood against the wall, *lehua* in natural green were wired with red flowers, baskets of *kupukupu* fern hung from the ceiling, garlands of fern crisscrossed against the ceiling, pillars were woven with *palapalai, wawaeiole,* and *uluhe* ferns accented with spikes of *ieie,* a form of *pandanus.* In the wide entrance hall, long tables were set with red cloths, huge platters of fresh fruit, and bowls of punch. Outside, the wide veranda was festooned with lit paper lanterns, and lehua sprayed with white and bright with red blossoms framed the entrance.

As the girls came down the stairway, Colonel Preston was in the center hall, giving directions to one of the manservants. When he looked up and saw his daughter, he stopped midsentence. For a moment he seemed stunned. He shook his head as if in disbelief. Then slowly a smile broke across his craggy face. He came to the foot of the steps and held out his hand. As she reached the last step, Edith took it and he spun her around a couple of times, declaring, "Darling girl, you are a vision to behold."

Jana halted a step or two behind Edith, saw the Colonel's eyes moisten. She knew he must be thinking of the young wife he had loved so much and had lost when Edith was a baby. An interesting reversal; the Hawaiian lady in a Paris gown and her daughter, a *hapa-haole*, who longed to claim her Hawaiian heritage.

Colonel Preston quickly controlled his momentary emotion and turned to Jana to graciously compliment her as well. "You two will have the young gentlemen battling to be your dance partners," he teased. "Jana, you'll have to excuse Edith for a while. She must do her duty in the receiving line with Bayard and me. I'm sure you won't find yourself alone for long. Bayard's guests have been impatiently waiting for you to appear." Jana watched as Edith gracefully picked up her train, took her father's arm, and went with him to greet the guests, who were arriving in a steady stream. Bayard was already standing at the door. His eyes swept over his sister. An enigmatic expression passed over his face. One Jana couldn't read. Disapproval? Amusement? Before she could interpret his gaze, he turned to her. He gave a nod and smiled. Again it was hard to know what his look meant.

Nor did she want to try. Bayard was someone she would never understand. Where had he been throughout the rodeo? She had seen him later with his father in what appeared to be a heated argument. Had Colonel Preston expected his son to ride and been disappointed he hadn't? It was hard to tell. Whatever it was, their discussion had ended abruptly, with both men walking away from each other, shoulders stiff.

Jana walked toward the drawing room, which had been transformed into a ballroom. Most of the formal furniture had disappeared mysteriously, the rugs had been rolled up, and the floor had been highly polished for dancing. The women guests were beautifully dressed. The parade of jewels and finery was overwhelming. There were enough ruffles, flounces, bows, bustles, ostrich feathers, fine laces, ivory fans, and ornamental combs to tax the vocabularies of the island's society page editors.

The sounds of the party swirled around Jana: the clinking of glasses, the murmur of conversation, the small bursts of laughter. It was a dizzying montage of movement and color. Menservants in bright, flowered shirts and white pants circulated with trays of iced tea or poured sparkling wine into crystal glasses never allowed to empty. A band of Hawaiian musicians in floral shirts and wearing *maile* — a fragrant, leafy vine — and leis were seated at one end of the large room. Their mellow guitars, backed by muted drums and the plink of ukuleles, provided a background of soft, melodic sound.

It was a dazzling scene that gave Jana a feeling of unreality, as though she were watching a colorful pageant, not being part of it. Then a voice at her side spoke.

"Good evening, Miss Rutherford." It was Joel. "You look lovely."

"Mahalo, thank you. It's borrowed. A fairy godmother waved a magic wand over me and — poof! — here I am," she laughed.

Joel shook his head. "You amaze me.

You're so natural, it's refreshing. Most girls simper when paid a compliment and start to fuss and fiddle with their hair or dress. I find it totally charming."

"To be honest, I have no idea how other girls act under these circumstances. It's the first time I've ever been to such a ball. I *do* feel like Cinderella."

"Would you like to dance?" he smiled.

"Yes. Edith and I have been practicing for weeks for just such a chance." Jana replied and let him lead her out onto the dance floor.

With a few false starts they got in step, and within minutes Jana was having the time of her life. Every once in a while she caught a glimpse of herself in the wall mirror. It was like looking at someone else. As Joel whirled her around in time to the music, the dress caught the light, and its fluttering ruffles edged with beading sparkled.

She and Joel were chatting between sets when Bayard's stint in the receiving line was evidently over, and he came up to them. "Come now, Joel, you cannot monopolize Jana all evening. Give someone else a turn, old fellow."

"Reluctantly," said Joel good-naturedly and left. When the music began again, Bayard held out his arms and Jana moved into them.

He danced as well as he rode, she thought, with skill and confidence. They circled the room three or four times, then reversed. But before she realized what he was doing, he had smoothly danced over to the open French windows and out onto the lanai. The night air was warm, balmy, scented. His hand circling her waist dropped to capture her hand. They walked to the edge, where the camellia bushes rimmed the terraced wall. He plucked a creamy blossom from its stem and handed it to her.

Jana took the flower, lifting it to her nose and inhaling the heavy sweetness of its fragrance. The only noise was the distant sound of the surf, the whisper of palm fronds crackling softly in the wind. Then Bayard spoke.

"Just one question. Was the gallant paniolo just playing a role this morning, or is he truly your cavalier?"

Surprised at his directness, Jana hesitated. Her truth might be one-sided. She had not yet talked to Kimo since the incident at the rodeo, had not yet discovered what he had meant when he handed her his ribbon. She couldn't be sure it meant what she hoped. Why did Bayard want to know? Why should she tell him? As her hesitation lengthened, Bayard gave a short laugh. "So is the old saying true? 'Silence gives consent'?"

"Not exactly. I don't know how to answer," she said quietly. "That paniolo was Kimo Kipola. Akela's cousin. I think you knew him — at least, as a boy. He's been away. On Oahu, at the Heritage Academy."

"Oh, an alli, then. Not just a cowboy. He rides like a seasoned paniolo."

"But then, so do *you*."

"We islanders —," he began, but a peal of laughter broke in on them as Edith and Tom and several other couples burst out from the ballroom. It was intermission, and the dancers were flocking out to the lanai to enjoy the cool ocean breeze.

There was no opportunity to continue the conversation. Actually, it had not been so much a conversation as an *interrogation* of her by Bayard. She was glad it had not continued. Why should she expose her heart to his razor-sharp wit? Why hand over her secret for him to examine, maybe ridicule? No. Jana had no intention of confiding in Bayard Preston.

The waiters followed the dancers out, bringing trays holding cups of cool punch for refreshment between dances. Joel had again engaged Jana's attention, and she was soon chatting with the others. When the music started playing again, Joel claimed her for the next set.

As the dancing continued, Jana had many partners. Even Greg Amory asked her to dance, and she found he was more pleasant than she had previously thought.

Ten minutes before midnight, the band stopped. Colonel Preston held up his hands for silence. "Time to see the new year in. Everyone is invited to come outside, and we'll see the old year out with a fine farewell, and the new one in with a howdy-do. Come along, we'll give 1886 a rousing welcome."

Jana knew from past years that Colonel Preston always put on an extravagant fireworks display that lit up the sky in celebration.

As brilliant, colorful bursts of scattering lights spun out in beautiful arcs against the dark sky, there were oohs and aahs of wonder. Then everyone joined in the slowly chanted countdown to midnight, until at last came the exuberant shout, "Happy New Year!"

Jana had been so entranced watching the fireworks, she did not notice that Bayard was standing behind her until the new year was announced. All around her, happy wishes and kisses were exchanged. She felt his arm go around her waist, and he turned her around, drew her close. *"Hau'oli Maka-*

hiki Hou," he whispered. Before she could draw back, his lips had found her mouth, in a kiss far more intense than a friendly New Year's greeting.

Jana was too startled to react at first. Besides, Bayard was holding her too tightly for her to easily escape his embrace. Underneath the happy voices and laughter, he said, "I had no idea you would grow up to be so irresistible."

Jana gave him a gentle push and stepped back, breathless, a little dizzy. Before she could think of a reply, Joel came up, said, "Happy New Year, Jana," and kissed her lightly. When she looked, Bayard had slipped away into the group around her. Tom and Greg and Edith followed, all laughing and happily exchanging kisses and greetings. Minutes later, Colonel Preston was inviting everyone to go inside again and toast the new year with a freshly uncorked bottle of champagne.

Although on the surface Jana joined with the others in the lighthearted chatter, inside she was a little shaken. Maybe when she was twelve or so, attention from Edith's older brother might have sent her head whirling, her heart thudding. Now it only troubled her. Now Kimo was back on the island. She had yet to discover if he loved her. Until she knew how Kimo felt toward her, she could not have any romantic feelings toward anyone else.

By one o'clock the party had dwindled. Most of the guests had departed after being served a sumptuous buffet. A few remained, gathered in clusters of conversation, some continuing to dance until the sleepy musicians packed up their instruments and prepared to leave.

Edith, as effervescent as each new bottle of champagne that Colonel Preston opened, was still dancing with a succession of partners.

Bayard had left to escort some of his father's guests who were staying over, down to the cottages. Jana and Joel sat near the open lanai doors, enjoying plates of fluffy scrambled eggs, banana nut bread, and cups of black, steaming Kona coffee. Greg Amory joined them. He looked around the room, commenting, "Look at this place! What a mess."

The other two followed his glance. Everywhere were the scattered remains of the party. The confetti that had been tossed out at midnight lay in crumpled streams of colors on the floor, wilting flowers hung limply where they had been festooned, the ribbons draped above the windows drooped gaudily in the light edging in through the windows.

"I'd sure hate to be on the cleanup committee," Joel laughed. "That's usually where I land after dances at our fraternity house."

"But you're in Hawaii," Jana reminded him. "Maybe the *menehuenes* will come and do it all."

"*Menehuenes?*" Greg echoed.

"Yes. The legendary 'little people' of the islands. You know, like Irish leprechauns or the trolls in Scandinavia? You've heard of *them*, haven't you?" Joel asked, eyes twinkling with the newly gained authority he had from Jana's coaching. "Well, the *menehuenes* are something like that. They build, do all sorts of mysterious things. They're said to appear only at night — but many claim to see them even in broad daylight."

"Come on!" Greg gave Joel a withering look. "Where did you get that kind of foolishness?"

"From an expert on Hawaii," Joel grinned.

Greg glanced at Jana. "*You?*"

"Yes, *me!*" she retorted. "And I get my information from the people who should know — the old ones, the *Kama'aina*." She looked Greg square in the eye. "There is so much about Hawaii that people don't know and outsiders don't understand," she said, hoping to beat him at his own game with her dismissing tone. However, it seemed to just whet Greg's appetite for baiting.

"You don't really believe all this stuff, do you?" Greg asked skeptically. "I mean, about Pele and the volcano and these — what did you call them, menehuenes?" Without waiting for her answer, Greg went on. "It's positively uncanny how primitive it all is under the surface." He halted, daring Jana to respond. "You seem like an intelligent girl. How can you stand — don't you ever want to see any place else? I mean, it's so limited here, so provincial — aren't you curious about the rest of the civilized world?"

Jana was ready to launch into a heated defense, when Colonel Preston walked over to make sure they were getting enough to eat, having a good time. The argument was immediately dropped.

In the absence of the band, Edith and Tom were seated at the piano, playing a lively tune, singing a duet. Some of the others, who'd thought they had run out of energy, now gathered around the piano.

Colonel Preston studied his daughter with pleasure. She was impetuous, stubborn, but also completely charming. There were only brief flashes when he saw his beautiful second wife in her. A momentary twinge of sadness and regret tugged at his heart as he remembered the serene, lovely, dark-eyed beauty who had been Edith's mother. The woman who had given him nothing but joy had left a daughter both headstrong and reckless who might one day be a problem. Still, his pride in his daughter was boundless.

"Edith lights up any room," Colonel Preston remarked almost to himself, then turned to Jana. "You've heard of people who march to a different drummer. . . . Edith dances to a melody no one else can hear."

It seemed a surprisingly lyrical observation for such a pragmatic man to make. Yet it was true. Edith had something quite unique, both the look of an American girl and the exotic beauty inherited from her Hawaiian mother.

Colonel Preston got to his feet. "I hope nothing changes her, takes that glow. I know that's wishful thinking. Whether we like it or not, whether we want it or not, life is a constant change. As the saying goes, 'One cannot hold back the dawn.' " He smiled at Jana. "And speaking of dawn, I have to admit that my old bones have just about had it. I'll leave you young ones to see in the first morning of the new year. I'm going to call it a night."

With a courtly bow he left, walking as steadily and straight as if he had not consumed a great quantity of the vintage champagne he had been urging on everyone else. The three of them watched him leave. Greg nodded his head in the direction of the piano, where Edith was still holding forth. "*She's* certainly the apple of his eye, isn't she? His little princess that nothing's too good for, right?"

"Well, I suppose so," Jana replied. "She *is* his only daughter — naturally he would dote on her."

"Oh, that's obvious. And she *is* a stunner. Especially in that Hawaiian outfit she's wearing tonight." He squinted his eyes slightly. He turned to Jana and said seriously, "There are subtle dangers in being brought up to believe you're special. There's danger for others as well — being lured into so much brilliance. Like moths drawn to the flame, there's a real possibility of being consumed."

It seemed a strange comment, when Jana knew *he* was the object of Edith's shining. Was he actively resisting her flame?

Suddenly she felt very tired. "I think I'll

say good night," she said and stood up. Joel stood up, too, and walked with her out to the hall.

At the bottom of the staircase, he said, "I've enjoyed being with you. You've made this vacation special, Jana. I hope we'll meet again — sometime."

"You'll come back to Hawaii. People usually do."

"I hope to."

He seemed to be about to say something else, but Jana said good night and went quickly upstairs.

She took off her borrowed finery, returned the gown to Edith's room, and replaced the dancing slippers, a little worse for wear. Edith's bed had been turned down, her nightgown and robe laid out for her, a thermos jug placed on the bedside table. Her every need, every wish, anticipated, taken care of — a princess indeed, just as Greg had commented. Looking around for a moment, Jana became newly aware of the difference between Edith's home life and her own. She had been here only a few days, and yet she realized how easy it would be to be seduced by all this luxury. When you were with the Prestons — any of them, the Colonel, Bayard, or Edith — there was this feeling that life was to be enjoyed fully, with no thought of tomorrow. It was such a contrast to how life was lived in her own home. Her parents, while not at all stuffy or overly strict, were both idealistic and high principled. They believed that the purpose of life was not merely to be happy, but to contribute something, to do something worthwhile, something that mattered. To find God's will for your life, was the important thing.

In his own words, all Colonel Preston wanted was for Edith to be happy. And what about Bayard? Did Colonel Preston expect more of his son? Probably. One day all this would belong to Bayard. A crown prince to take over the kingdom.

Back in the guest room, Jana put the gardenia Bayard had given her into the small crystal vase beside the bed. She thought of the intensity of his kiss. . . . What should she make of it?

This room overlooked the lanai, from which the murmur of voices and the laughter of the group who still lingered rose. Someone was singing a familiar Hawaiian melody, accompanied by the sweet plink of a ukulele. The sounds mingled dreamily as she drifted off.

For her the party had ended. The holidays were over. It had been an exciting interlude. But that's all it had been.

Chapter 9

Jana was not sure how long she had been asleep when suddenly, slashing through her dreams, came Bayard's harsh command, *"Get to bed, Edith!"*

Instantly awake, Jana sat bolt upright in bed, every nerve tingling. She strained to listen for what might follow. But she could hear nothing more. Only dead silence. The loudest sound was her own heart hammering. She reached for the small clock on the bedside table. After three! She had left the party little more than an hour ago. What had happened since then? What had Edith done to cause her brother to shout at her like that?

She only had to wait minutes to find out. She heard running feet along the corridor outside her room, and then the door burst open and Edith ran in, flung herself, sobbing, onto Jana's bed.

Jana put her arms around her friend's violently shaking shoulders. Frightened, she held her while the wrenching sobs went on and on. Bayard adored his little sister, treated her with affectionate indulgence. What kind of quarrel had erupted between them to bring on *this?*

Gradually the gulping sobs lessened, the ragged breaths became gasps. Finally Edith sat up, wiping her eyes with her fists like a child, and found her voice.

"I'll never forgive him! Never!" she said fiercely between clenched teeth.

"Kiki, tell me! What happened?"

"I'm furious! How could Bayard humiliate me that way? I didn't do anything wrong! He just . . . just *assumed* . . . oh, I don't know what! It was beastly of him."

"Calm down, please. Just tell me what happened."

Edith gulped. "I need a hankie."

"Here, use this!" Jana lifted the bud vase in which she had put her gardenia and slipped the lace-edged doily from under it and handed it to Edith. "Now *tell* me."

"Well . . . ," she began, then sniffled and blew her nose before going on. "Only a few of us were left — actually me, Greg, Tom, and Joel. You know how interested *he* is in everything about Hawaii, asking all sorts of questions — about the native customs and so on. He asked about Hawaiian music, so I picked up a ukulele and was playing some of the tunes we all know. He liked one particularly and I told him it was one the *hula* was danced to. Well, one thing led to another, and I decided to show him what a hula was. I took off my shoes" — Edith pulled up her skirt and stuck out her legs, wiggling bare feet — "and I began to dance for him. I was telling one of the island legends, the way Akela's mother taught us, and I was just doing it, when all of a sudden Bayard came thundering out onto the lanai and shouted at me!"

"And that's all? That's *it?*"

Edith nodded. "I don't know what got into him or what he thought I was doing — but I've never seen him so angry. I was shocked. Totally stunned. I dropped the ukulele and ran into the house." She sniffed again. "I don't know what the others thought. Or how Bayard will explain himself to his friends." Edith thumped a fist on the edge of the mattress. "Oh, it was unspeakable! I'll never forgive him for shaming me like that — in front of everyone. Especially *Greg!*"

"Oh, Kiki," Jana said, attempting to soothe her. "It will probably all blow over. In the morning, everyone will have forgotten it."

"I won't have," Edith said stubbornly.

"Bayard will be sorry," Jana assured her. "I'm sure he would never intentionally hurt you." Then she added as an afterthought, "You know, everyone had a great deal of champagne. . . ." This, she knew, was rather a lame excuse. She had the feeling it wasn't too much champagne that had made Bayard lash out at his sister. It was more probably his own internal conflicts.

It was a long time before Edith stopped railing at her brother. After a while she seemed to go limp.

"Things will look better tomorrow. You'll see, Kiki."

"I don't know how," Edith sighed.

"I'm sure Bayard will apologize and everything will be fine."

"Maybe," Edith said doubtfully. "I hope you're right."

At length she got off the bed, said a sleepy good night, and went listlessly into her adjoining bedroom.

Jana had trouble getting back to sleep. What a shame, she thought, that the beautiful party and the celebration of the start of a new year had ended so badly.

After Edith left, Jana lay awake. She realized there was deeply felt bitterness in Bayard Preston. He was caught between two cultures. As Colonel Preston's son by his marriage to an American woman, he was ever considered by Hawaiians as a *haole*. No matter that he had been born here on the island. His was a love-hate relationship with the island. Half the year, he lived in the United States, where Hawaii was considered a foreign country, its traditions trivialized, its legends and lovely customs vulgarized. He managed to keep his anger controlled and suppressed — most of the time — but it cost him.

Jana understood that under his outburst at his sister's dancing was his fear that his friends would consider the hula something pagan, uncivilized. After all, the first missionaries had banned it at one time. They had missed the significance of the graceful, legend-telling native dance. He had impulsively acted in defense of what he held dear — Hawaii and Edith.

It was a long time before Jana's troubling thoughts allowed her to go to sleep again.

The sun streaming in through the latticed screens awoke Jana. She lay there for a moment, reluctant to come into full wakefulness. The bed felt soft, comforting, like a cocoon from which she did not want to pull herself. But slowly the events of the ball and the aftermath pulled her into consciousness.

She hoped there would be no repercussions from the upsetting scene between Bayard and Edith last night. She slipped out of bed and went over to the windows to see what kind of day the weather promised for the garden party planned as the last event of the holiday. Stepping out onto the balcony, she heard Bayard's and Colonel Preston's voices from the lanai below. Bayard was speaking earnestly.

"Father, I know it would be hard for you to let her go. But Edith needs exposure to another culture, to the society in which she should learn to move, behave. You must see that, Father. She's grown up almost wild here. She knows nothing but this island, the provincial attitudes. She needs polishing. She needs a whole other environment, different friends, other influences — she needs to associate with people of our own class, not just Hawaiians."

Jana stepped back as if she had been slapped. Bayard's words "not just Hawaiians," stung. Did he include *her* when he said Edith needed a different kind of friends?

The night before, she had felt compassion for his uncertainty about his life, had felt she understood it. Now she had only resentment, anger. Jana started to go back inside, but something held her. Colonel Preston was protesting.

"I can't let her go so far away."

"I'm not talking about England or a French finishing school, Father. There are many fine finishing schools in New England near New Haven, where she could be close enough to Yale so I could see her. Every weekend, if it came to that. And you could visit often. You make at least one trip to the States every year as it is." Bayard paused, then said more forcefully, "Believe me, Father, it's for Edith's own good. At least promise you'll think about it, won't you?" Another pause. "In the meantime, I'll do some checking into some of the schools for young ladies in the States."

Suddenly Jana wished she had not overheard this conversation. The bright promise of the day ahead faded. She wished she could leave the ranch. Right away. Go home. She was hurt. Words were weapons that could wound. The cuts Bayard's words had inflicted were deep. And they were ones from which she might not recover.

The two men's voices faded as they left the lanai. Later she heard the sound of their horses' hooves as they rode down the drive for an early morning horseback ride together. Jana dressed quickly and went downstairs. No one else seemed to be up or around except Meipala, who told her with a wink that the other guests were still sleeping, adding with a chuckle, "It musta been some *okolehao*." Silently agreeing and secretly glad to be alone, Jana took her coffee out to the lanai to drink, in case one of the young men took it into their heads to come up to the big house for breakfast. She wasn't in the mood to socialize.

The prospect of the garden party loomed ahead. It was Colonel Preston's annual open house to his local friends on New Year's Day. New year, Jana thought, sighing. What did this new year hold for her? By this time next year, she would be almost through high school, and maybe even accepted at some mainland college and selected to receive a scholarship, if her parents' hopes were fulfilled. The prospect filled her with sadness. She didn't really want to go to the mainland. Unlike Bayard, she loved her life here — she didn't want anything to change. His words to his father came back to her now, and she felt the slow rise of resentment again. There was still the garden party to get through. She would make it a point to avoid Bayard at this afternoon's party. If she didn't, she might lose her temper and tell him what she thought of his attitude about

Hawaii and Hawaiians!

Jana finished her coffee and went back inside and upstairs. Edith was awake and last night's trauma seemed to have dimmed sufficiently for her to be her usual cheerful self. She had always been able to throw off moods, dismiss unpleasant situations. Surprisingly, she seemed to hold no grudge against her brother. In fact, she did not even mention what had happened the night before. She was flitting around her room like a butterfly, trying on one dress after the other to wear to the afternoon party.

While Edith seemed to be looking forward to it, Jana dreaded it. But there was no way to escape. She just hoped her father would come early to pick her up and take her home.

That afternoon, the garden was soon filled with ladies in pastel gowns and gentlemen in white linen suits, arriving from Hilo and Kona in their splendid carriages. While Edith moved gaily about among the guests, laughing and chatting and showing off one of the flowered organdy gowns her aunt had sent, Jana tried to be as inconspicuous as possible.

Her effort to avoid Bayard proved impossible. She was hovering near the punch bowl, thinking herself safe, when she felt a hand on her waist gently but insistently turn her around and she was face to face with him.

"Why are you running away from me?" he asked.

Disconcerted, Jana demanded, "What makes you think that?"

"It's pretty obvious."

Remembering how Edith had often told her Bayard was *pursued* by young ladies in the most blatant fashion, Jana wanted to say something to deflate his smug assertion. "You're pretty self-important to think I would go to the bother."

For a minute he seemed taken aback. "I was under the impression that we were *hoalohas*, friends, that we understood one another." He frowned. "Was I wrong?"

"I don't know, I'm sure," Jana shrugged.

"I thought your lack of artifice, flirtatiousness, was very attractive. I don't like to see you playing the usual feminine games."

"Don't be so patronizing," she flashed back at him. "Not every girl in the world wants to fall at your feet."

Bayard's eyes narrowed, his mouth tightened. Then he did a surprising thing. He reached his hand under her chin, tilted it upward with his fingertips, gazing into her eyes.

"I'm disappointed in you, Jana. I thought you were different. I guess I was mistaken."

She felt her cheeks burn. Her first indignation began suddenly to dissipate. A smile touched Bayard's lips, as if he had read her thoughts or had found out what he wanted to know. His hand dropped away from her and he stepped back.

"It's all right, Jana. Forget what I said. Forget everything." With that he turned and walked away.

Jana got through the rest of the afternoon trying to follow Bayard's suggestion. To forget the whole incident. Still, it cast its shadow. She was relieved when her father arrived earlier than expected to take her home.

Chapter 10

Jana was glad to be home. The house party had been like indulging in too much rich food — she was happy to be back in her familiar surroundings, eating the plain fare of her regular life again.

Most of all, she hoped the Kipolas were back from Kona and that Kimo would come to see her. After being exposed to Bayard and his college friends, it would be wonderful to be with someone like Kimo. So natural, so honest, so completely who he was.

Remembering how his eyes had lit up when he first greeted her outside the church that evening before Christmas, and the way he had looked at her as he handed her his scarf at the rodeo, had sent her hopes soaring.

Her mother wanted to hear all the details of the house party. Jana tried to give her a full report, except she left out the part about the borrowed designer gown she'd substituted for her own to wear to the New Year's Eve ball. She didn't want to hurt her mother's feelings, so to distract her from questions about what *she* had worn, Jana went into great detail about Edith's Hawaiian dress. She also left out her strange encounters with Bayard. Jana had the impression her mother would not have approved at all of any of it.

Her mother seemed satisfied with the account. "Well, I'm glad you had a good time, dear."

Two days later, Jana took Nathan down to the beach to play.

She was helping him build a sand fort when she happened to look up and see a tall, familiar figure coming along the beach toward them.

"Look, Jana. It's Kimo!" exclaimed Nathan, dropping his little shovel and waving his hand.

Kimo waved back. He came up to them as casually as if he had never been away at all. "Aloha." His gaze met Jana's over Nathan's head. Then, smiling, he squatted down on the sand beside Nathan, started scooping sand, packing it along with him. In a minute he looked up and grinned at Jana.

"Like old times, eh?"

"Yes," she smiled, "like old times."

It was as simple as that. Even Nathan seemed to accept Kimo's presence, as if it had only been a matter of days since they were all together. Later, when Nathan was busily running back and forth to the shallows to fill his sand bucket with water and bring it back up to fill the moat they had constructed around his fortress, Kimo and Jana began to talk.

"I loved getting your letters," he told her. "It was like receiving a piece of home. I could almost see, hear, and taste Hawaii." He smiled. "Mahalo."

"I'm glad. I liked writing them." She paused, hardly daring to meet his gaze, and then she said shyly, "I missed you." She quickly asked, "How did you happen to come to the rodeo?"

"One of my cousins is a paniolo, works for the Preston Ranch." There was a slight sharpness to his saying of the name Preston — or was it her imagination? "He told me about it, said there were always prizes, that it would be fun. So I thought, why not?" Kimo shrugged. "Truthfully, Akela told me you would be at the ranch for their New Year's celebration, so I decided to come along, hoped I might see you."

Ah, what she had longed to know, but to hide the color she felt flaming into her cheeks, Jana ducked her head as though to dampen down a crack in one of the fort's turrets with water Nathan had just dumped into a hole at her feet.

"Well, you did," she murmured.

"Yes, and it was wonderful," Kimo said quietly.

Jana raised her head and looked straight at him. This was how it should be. No games, no teasing, no subtle playing. Kimo didn't know the meaning of subterfuge. What a relief. He was telling her he missed her and that he cared. Now she was free to do the same.

"Oh Kimo, I'm so glad to see you. How long will you be here?"

"Another week. You know this is my last year at the academy. My teachers have suggested I apply for an apprenticeship to a famous cabinetmaker in Germany —"

"Germany!" Jana gasped. She had forgotten all about the possiblity that Kimo would receive the apprenticeship. She vaguely remembered him talking about it. But that had been long ago. So many other things had happened since she had first heard about it. But no . . . She blinked. The thought of Kimo's leaving struck with a sharp pain.

"Yes. He is very well known. One of the finest. It would be a real honor to be accepted. He only accepts a limited number of apprentices."

"But it's so far away! So far from Hawaii."

"Yes, I know. But it would mean so much. Everything. For the future. If I get the opportunity, when I come back I can start my own business."

Over the hard lump rising in her throat, Jana managed to ask, "How long would you be gone?"

"Two years."

"Two years?" she repeated, her heart sinking.

Kimo met her startled eyes.

"You would care? That I was gone?"

"Yes, of course." She lowered her eyes, afraid he would see the sadness and the fear in them. Fear that if he were gone that long, he might forget her. . . .

"No, Koana," he said softly. "Don't look so sad. It is such an opportunity for me, for the future. If I get to go — well then, I must go." He paused. "You'll be going off to school next year, too, won't you? Akela tells me your parents want you to go to teachers college in the States."

"Yes, but I —" Jana made a sweeping fan in the sand with one hand, saying almost defiantly, "I don't want to go! All I ever want is to stay here and paint!"

Nathan, who had kept busy building his fort, suddenly looked up and said, "Jana's an artist. She paints really good. Did you know that, Kimo?"

Kimo laughed and reached his hand out, tousling the little boy's hair. "Yes, I knew that, *keiki*. She sent me some of her paintings when I was away." He turned back to Jana. "That's what you will do, Koana. First you will do what your parents wish, and then you'll come back here and paint." He added softly, "Maybe we both have to go away — to come back."

For a moment Jana looked into Kimo's eyes and knew that what had passed between them was real, binding, and a promise. A promise that couldn't be spoken of yet, but one they both understood.

Kimo got to his feet. "I'm taking Tutu over to Aunt Peula's this evening. But could we spend tomorrow together? Take a picnic somewhere?"

"Oh yes, I'd like that," Jana answered, feeling her heart rise happily.

"Well then, I'll be on my way," he said. "Aloha, Nakana."

The little boy looked up and grinned. "Aloha, Kimo."

"Aloha, Koana," Kimo said to Jana, who echoed, "Aloha."

Kimo left then and walked back down the beach the way he'd come, stopping halfway, turning back to wave his hand. Waving hers in return, Jana felt happiness flood all through her. Kimo was back. He'd come home and to her. Just as she'd dreamed, just as she'd prayed.

The next day when Kimo came, Jana was waiting. She had to check her impatience while he carried on a leisurely conversation with her parents. He answered her father's questions — about school, his classes, his woodworking, life at the Heritage Academy — seemingly in no hurry.

At length Jana picked up the picnic basket she'd packed early, and moved to the top of the porch steps. Her mother took the hint and said, "Well, you two have a nice day." As they went down the steps, she cautioned, "Jana, be sure to keep your hat on. You know how freckled you get with too much sun."

Inwardly Jana winced. Why did her mother have to remind her — and Kimo too — that hers was not the sun-loving skin of a Hawaiian girl?

"Yes, ma'am," she replied.

Kimo threw her a teasing glance, then said to her mother, "I'll see that she doesn't get sunburned, Mrs. Rutherford."

They took the path behind the house that led to the beach. Jana remembered the days when she and Kimo had raced down this same way when they were children. So many shared times, so many happy memories.

"Akela should be here!" she said impulsively.

"She's with Pelo. She stayed over in Kona for a few days so that she could be with him some more."

Jana stopped in her tracks, surprised, and looked questioningly at Kimo. He smiled. "I think they're in love," he said matter-of-factly.

"Oh?"

"Yes. Don't look so surprised. It happens."

"Of course. I know, it's just that —"

"Akela didn't say anything to you? Well, she's shy. It's easy to tell when they're together. They have eyes only for each other."

When they got to the beach, they found a nice sheltered spot under a banyan tree, surrounded by dunes, and set down the basket.

"So did you have a good time at the Prestons' house party?" he asked her.

How to describe all that had happened? "It was all right. But —" Suddenly Jana decided this might be the time to ask him about the night outside the church when he first came home. Hesitantly she told him how she felt, saying, "I thought you were angry at me."

"Angry? No, I'd never be angry at *you*, Koana. I guess I was just disappointed that you'd be away when I got back from Kona. Besides, maybe I resent the Prestons a little. For a lot of reasons that have nothing to do with you. *Kala mai ia'u,* I'm sorry, if you misunderstood."

Relieved, Jana said impulsively, "I'm glad. I was afraid something had happened that we wouldn't be — well, friends anymore."

Kimo reached for her hand, held it for a minute. "We'll always be friends, Koana, re-member?" Then he leaned forward and with his finger wrote something in the sand — *kau a kau maka maka,* forever friends.

Reading what he had written, Jana felt a warmth spread all through her until her very fingertips tingled. "Mahalo," she said, smiling.

"Let's walk down where the rocks are, look for tide pools," he suggested, getting to his feet, then reaching down to take her hand and pull her to her feet.

"Wait!" she said and bent to unlace her shoes, pull off her stockings. Kimo had al-ready kicked off his sandals. Together they walked to the edge of the water and waded along the shallows, letting the incoming tide curl around their bare feet.

"Tell me about Honolulu," Jana demanded. "Did you ever see the king?"

"The 'Merry Monarch'? Not often. We heard a great deal about him. The Iolani Palace is beautiful — at least, that's what people say. I can't, because I've never been invited there myself."

"You're entitled, though, aren't you? I mean, being that you're a descendant of one of the chieftains of Hawaii?"

"So are many students at our school. Queen Kapiolani attended the graduation and awards day at the academy. But I was sitting too far away to get a good look at her. The girls said she was gorgeously dressed, silken trains swishing, jewels sparkling. The king is supposed to be something to see, too," Kimo laughed. "He has so many medals on his uniform, people have to shield their eyes, because the sun makes them dazzling."

"That sounds so exciting. Seeing royalty and all. Tell me more," Jana begged.

"I've heard other things about the king, but I don't know whether I should tell you or not. You're such an innocent," he teased.

"I am not!" she retorted indignantly. "Tell me, please. You must," she pleaded.

"Well, you've heard that the Scottish poet

Robert Louis Stevenson is a great friend of the king's. He visits the palace often, and they spend lots of time together."

"That's all? Why shouldn't you tell me that?"

"You interrupted me. I was going to say that rumor has it he puts away four or five bottles of champagne in an afternoon. However, Stevenson says the king is none the worse for it. If you can believe that. Stevenson also declares that King Kalakua is very fine and intelligent. You knew he was an accomplished musician and composer, didn't you?"

"All Hawaiians are talented," Jana said. "*You* are."

"With my hands," Kimo conceded. "That's not like hearing music in your head and being able to put it into notes so other people can play it on instruments or sing the words."

"You make beautiful things out of wood. Just like poets make something beautiful with words," Jana insisted. "Poetry in wood."

"Mahalo," Kimo said quietly. "I'll remember that."

That day together was one Jana would treasure for a long time after Kimo had returned to Honolulu. She was so happy, in a way that was different from other times of happiness. With Kimo she was more truly herself than with anyone else. There was no need for explanations, not even for words.

In the week that followed, they saw each other almost every day. When Akela came back from Kona to Tutu's, they made a threesome, often taking Nathan along with them on their picnics and sometimes sailing. Kimo was teaching Jana's little brother to swim and surf, and those were wonderful days.

Then at last it was time for Kimo to return to Honolulu. The afternoon before he was to leave the next morning, Kimo came alone to walk with Jana along the ocean.

They both knew that something had happened, something had changed in their relationship. They were not children, not playmates, any longer — they were something more than friends. What they were now to each other, neither was quite able to say.

There was a certain poignancy to that last afternoon they spent together. They didn't talk much, just held hands and walked along the beach. As the wind off the ocean grew cool, the shadows long, they knew it was time to go. Before leaving the beach, Kimo halted by the surf's edge, sat down on his heels, and wrote something else in the wet sand. Jana leaned over to read the words *Aloha ka-ua,* Let there be love between you and me.

He stood up, looked at her with dark, serious eyes. Then he took her hand and they walked slowly up the path back to the Rutherfords' cottage.

At the gate Kimo asked, "Will you write to me, Koana?"

"You hardly ever answer," she pretended to pout.

"They keep us pretty busy at school. After classes there's workshop. Then we all have other duties around the grounds and buildings. Lots of work, not many hours to yourself. But I'll do better this year, I promise," he laughed softly. "I like getting your letters on that pretty pink stationery. I get a lot of joshing from the other fellows when they see those envelopes with the flowers you paint on them."

"Do you mind?"

"No, it makes me feel proud. Someone cares enough about me to take the time and trouble to write." He paused. "You do care, don't you, Koana?"

He had to bend his head to hear her reply, "Yes, I do."

Then Kimo put his hands on her shoulders, leaned forward, and kissed her on both cheeks, the traditional Hawaiian way. "Aloha, Koana."

Impulsively Jana put her hands up, captured his face in them, held it for a moment, then kissed him on the mouth.

"Aloha, Kimo."

The day after Kimo left for Oahu again, Jana felt lonelier than she had ever remembered. The possibility that the next time Kimo left the island it might be for Germany made her desolate. Something had happened between them during this vacation, something new, something different. *Aloha kaua a kau maka maka.* She wrote those words over and over, on scrap paper and on the margins of her lined school tablet "may we be friends forever."

When school started again, Jana was shocked to learn from Edith that her father, acting upon Bayard's advice, was investigating schools on the mainland for her to attend next year. Dismayed, Jana exclaimed, "Then, you won't be graduating with Akela and me?"

"I know, I'm sorry about that. At first I told Papa I wouldn't go! Then he kept persuading me" — she dimpled — "*bribing* me, you might say. Adding things he would do if

I'd agree to go. He's even promised to ship Malakini to Walnut Hills for me to ride when I'm there. And Bayard says that's near enough to New York to go to the theater and go shopping at the big stores, and there'll be all sorts of interesting places to go and see. Besides parties and balls at the nearby men's college." Edith's eyes sparkled with excitement at the promise of a new life.

Jana did not say anything. She remembered Bayard's voice coming clearly to her from the patio on New Year's morning: ". . . she needs to associate with people of our own class, not just Hawaiians."

Part 2

Capter 11

September 1886

Edith left for the mainland to the fashionable boarding school she would be attending in Virginia. Jana and Akela accompanied her and the Colonel to Hilo to see them off on the steamer to Honolulu. The friends embraced and said tearful good-byes. Although Edith shed copious tears when she hugged them both, there was an unmistakable excitement in her farewells. As eager for new experiences as Edith was, this was the ultimate adventure for her.

As they stood on the dock watching the steamer move out of the harbor, a sense of melancholy hung over the two girls left behind. Riding back in the Prestons' carriage, they were somberly aware of the fact that the two of them would be starting their last year of high school without the third member of their trio. Although they didn't put it into words, both girls felt that something would definitely be missing in their lives.

The months that followed Edith's departure were even harder for Jana than for Akela. Jana felt Edith's absence more keenly than Akela did. Akela was always surrounded by the large, supportive Kipola family, with their frequent gatherings. Then too, she now had Pelo to love and comfort her. Almost every other weekend, Akela went to Kona to be near him.

Edith proved a poor correspondent. A month after she left, Jana and Akela received a letter addressed to them both, in which she described her life as "hectic" and said that the school kept them "hopping":

There are classes in everything you can imagine! Fencing! Dancing! French! Weekends, we have all sorts of social activities, such as the dansants (that's French, but means that young men from nearby schools come, stand against the wall, and gawk at us, then clumsily ask some of us to dance, and we all drink fruit punch). I live in a suite of six rooms. There are two girls to a room, and we share a sitting room. My roommate's name is Vinnie Albright.

That was about the extent of correspondence from Edith. She did, however, send picture postcards from many of the "educational" field trips the school took to "historic sites" — one a view of Mount Vernon, another of Jefferson's Monticello, yet another of the Washington Monument.

With both Edith and Kimo gone, Jana felt lonely. She missed Kimo especially and more than she had expected to. He had been gone all summer, working at a woodworker's shop in Manoa on Oahu. After their brief, idyllic reunion at the beginning of the year, she thought his feelings for her had changed, deepened, become more than just affection. Why hadn't he written? But then, why should she have thought he would? He had told her he wasn't good about writing.

However, it was a terrible blow when Jana learned that Kimo had been accepted as an apprentice by the German cabinetmaker. When Akela told her he would leave for Germany without returning to Hawaii, Jana was stunned. What had only been a possibility had become a reality. Germany was a world away. She couldn't share with anyone, not even Akela, how much it hurt that Kimo hadn't written to tell her himself. Her feelings for Kimo were buried deep in her secret heart.

Jana tried to fill up the emptiness she felt by concentrating on her studies and her painting. Still, her days seemed long and lonely. She took Nathan with her to the beach and sketched while he played, she helped her mother with household tasks, and somehow time passed.

Another disappointment came with the news that Edith would not come home for Christmas as they had all hoped. Instead, the Colonel would travel to the mainland, where Bayard would meet them in New York for a holiday of parties and theater-going. Edith had sent a hasty note of explanation along with presents for both her friends — a chiffon scarf for Akela, and a beaded evening purse for Jana. What possible use she would have for it, Jana didn't know. To make matters worse, Akela would be gone to Kona for the Kipolas' annual family gathering. As a result, Jana was hard put to pretend she was looking forward to Christmas. For Nathan's sake she tried.

As if to lighten her sagging sprits, a few days before Christmas she received a package in the mail. It was heavily wrapped in brown paper, with lots of strings and stamps. From Germany, from *Kimo!* Excitedly she unwrapped it and found a book of reproductions of lovely watercolors, pictures of Rhineland castles and cathedrals. Inside was a short letter saying that he was living with a German family, managing to learn enough of the language to get along, and that the cabinetmaker to whom he was apprenticed was a hard taskmaster and kept them working long hours.

I've never been good at putting thoughts into words, as you know, Koana, but I do think of you every day. I miss you. I miss our talks, our times together. I miss everything in Hawaii. It is so strange to be so far from everything I love and understand.

Jana read these few lines over and over. Was she included in those things Kimo loved and understood? In the note, Jana sensed the deep loneliness Kimo must be experiencing, and she wept sympathetic tears, feeling his heartache.

Spring 1887

With graduation only a few months away, Jana filled out several applications to a number of women's colleges. Her parents suggested one in San Francisco that offered a two-year course to earn a teacher's credential. There was a need for elementary teachers on the island, and finding a position would be almost guaranteed. Obediently but halfheartedly, Jana filled out the forms. She didn't want to teach — she wanted to be an artist. She had sent for the brochure of a California art school and had learned that there were scholarships available.

She had discovered Psalm 37, and it had become her favorite. Especially verses 3 and 4, which she said over and over to herself: "Trust in the Lord . . . Delight yourself also in him, and he will give you the desires of your heart." Why would the Lord have planted the desire to paint so deeply, given her the talent she had, if he didn't mean to "bring it to pass"?

The thought of going away from the island to the mainland was frightening. There had been so many changes in her life in such a short time — in the space of a year, actually — with both Edith's and Kimo's departures from Hawaii. Jana didn't want to leave the island, didn't feel ready for such a change. To be in a strange surrounding, among strangers, didn't appeal to her. Only if she could win a scholarship to an art school might the idea be more acceptable.

Then she could come back to Hawaii and fulfill her dream of being an artist, even if she had to teach to support herself.

To qualify for one she had to submit a portfolio of her artwork, with one main piece on which her chances for a scholarship would be decided. Both parents were full of suggestions. Her father liked many of the watercolor seascapes she had done, her mother favored copies she had made of famous paintings. Jana knew it should be something entirely original. She wanted to do something that would stand out from other entrants. Something that expressed her in a unique way. Something that spoke of Hawaii, that came from her heart, expressed her feelings. A personal statement. That was what she felt would attract the judges, the people who decided who got the scholarships.

Jana walked the beach, stared out her window, prayed about it, thought, sketched, and tore up many attempts before at last she got an idea. She would design a quilt, a pattern, blending both styles, Hawaiian and American, into one beautiful, complete design. Just as she herself was a blend of both cultures. Excited as she was about her idea, she knew she needed to learn more about the Hawaiian quilts. She decided to go talk to Tutu, who was always working on a quilt, and share her idea and find out about the "secret" hidden in Hawaiian quilts. She wanted her design to have its own secret meaning as well.

Tutu welcomed Jana as usual and was eager to share her wisdom and talent with her.

"We take quilt making very seriously in Hawaii," she began. "It is considered an art, an individual, creative expression of each woman," she said in her soft voice. "The missionary ladies taught Hawaiians to quilt and showed them how to cut out the patterns and sew them on the cloth. Gradually, instead of copying the designs the missionaries gave them, Hawaiian ladies began to create their own." Tutu's capable brown hands moved slowly, taking precise, small stitches. "My mother made beautiful quilts. She was a very spiritual lady. She prayed over her quilts, blessing the persons who would receive them as a gift, sleep under them." She paused, then went on thoughtfully. "Her designs were often the result of a vision or dream. An idea would come and she would cut it out from memory, with no pattern.

"The cloths used by the missionary ladies for bedcovers were much different from the ones Hawaiians used. In the olden days, people slept on mats woven from the *lauhala,* the ribbonlike leaves of the *pnadanus.* They were soft and fine, almost like silk to the touch. Before the missionaries came, Hawaiian women were skillful in making tapa cloth from the inner bark of the *wauke* plant. They wet it and shaped it into size, dried it in the sun, pounded it. It was a long, tedious process. Tapa cloth was then used for everything, for clothing as well as for bedcovers."

"But the quilts you make, Tutu, are constructed much like the ones my mother has, like the ones my grandmother makes. A padded undercloth, then the design part on top."

"Yes, I know. The basic quilt is the same. All of us who attended the missionary schools learned how to cut and sew and make quilts like we were taught. The difference is in the design. For some reason, we were quick to learn the skill of handling needle and thread and stitching the appliquéd patterns. The art was in creating our own designs."

Jana watched, fascinated, as Tutu's needle weaved in and out around the pattern she was applying to the quilt. It was the shape of a pineapple.

"Hawaiians took to quilt making very easily," Tutu went on. "Hawaiians love happy occasions and any reason to celebrate. They love to make gifts to give loved ones at special times, such as weddings, birthdays, new babies, and other joyful happenings. Quilts are perfect for this. My mother made wedding quilts for all her daughters and daughters-in-law, and many, many baby quilts." Tutu laughed her deep, throaty laugh.

"But what about the secret, Tutu? Tell me about them," Jana asked. She was curious about this element, which made the Hawaiian quilts different from the ones her mother's aunties had given her.

"Well, there's a code of ethics about the quilts. The person who creates a design keeps it a secret. To exchange an original design is a sign of a deep bond of friendship and is rarely done, but when it is, the person who receives the design alters it slightly to put her own stamp upon it and to respect the originator." Tutu halted, holding up the part she was working on, putting her head to one side, and studying it for a minute before continuing. "Even the giver of an original design does not necessarily confide the hidden inspiration of it to the person receiving it — that is her choice. Sometimes it is too personal or has such intimate meaning that she wants to keep it to herself. Often it could be a particular event, or a meaningful episode in her life, that she does not want to share with anyone."

Jana could understand that. In her mind, an idea for her "secret" message in her design was forming, and it was something she knew she wanted to keep private.

"What about the quilt you're making now, Tutu? Does it have a secret?"

"Aha, Koana — if I told you, it would no longer be a secret, would it?" she chuckled. "But no, this is one I'm making by request. My sister wanted me to make this one like one I made before. It's a more common design. Hawaii has so many beautiful flowers and fruits, most of the simpler designs are drawn from pineapple, breadfruit, and anthurium shapes. One of my personal favorites is a quilt I made after I was baptized."

"The one hanging in your bedroom on the wall opposite your bed?" Jana had often admired the colorful design of that one. With its orange-colored fruit, red flowers, and green foliage on a white background, it looked like a garden in full bloom.

"It reminds me of one of the happiest days of my life," Tutu smiled reminiscently. "I hung it there so I could see it every night before I go to sleep and it's the first thing I see in the morning when I wake up."

Jana knew that Tutu's religion meant everything to her. She could remember waking up early sometimes during the nights she spent with Akela and hearing Tutu praying. The cottage had an open floor plan, and from where Jana slept on a mat in Akela's bedroom, she could see Tutu standing at the window in the front of the house, looking out over the valley, holding her big, floppy Bible in both hands. Later when both girls were awake, Tutu always led them in grace before breakfast and always ended it with, "Today, Lord, I ask that you bless our day and let us be a blessing to others."

Jana had incorporated that thought into her own prayers.

"So, little one, have you heard enough about quilts for now?" Tutu asked, starting to fold up her work, signaling it was time for her to stop for the day.

"Yes. Mahalo, Tutu, you've helped me so much." Jana rose, then kissed Tutu's soft cheek and left.

On her way home Jana felt excited. She could not wait to get home, get out her drawing board, her sketch board and put the idea for a quilt design on paper.

Actually it was only after several sketches made, torn up, and begun again that finally Jana traced her design onto a sheet of fine watercolor paper and carefully outlined it.

Hawaiian quilts were always given a name as well as a secret title known only to the quilter. She wanted to choose an appropriate one for her design. That was a little longer in coming. As she selected the colors, she prayed to get just the right name, the one that was meaningful and true to what she wanted to express. The colors were easier, she used the yellow of the royal hibiscus, the violet blue of the jacaranda blossoms, and the pale pink of the anthuriums to represent what she found most beautiful about Hawaii — the flowers that grew here wild, as purely God's creation on this special island.

Hour after hour as she painted in the design the Scripture verse that came to her was Matthew 6:28. "Consider the lilies of the field . . . even Solomon in all his glory was not arrayed as one of these."

She didn't show it to anyone, didn't want anyone to see it until it was finished, until she was satisfied that it was the best work she could do.

At length as the deadline for submission for scholarship consideration neared, she allowed her parents to see it.

"It's lovely, darling," her mother said. "Just beautiful."

"Very fine, Jana. I'm proud of you, my dear," her father nodded. "And what do you call it?"

She told them she was going to letter in the Scripture verse with an explanatory note that the flowers depicted were all indigenous to the island.

"Good. I think the judges will take note of that." Her father seemed pleased.

The secret title she kept to herself, not sure anyone else would really understand. She called it *The Gift*. Because she felt being born in Hawaii was a gift, growing up here was a gift, her talent was a gift. And she wanted the design, whether it won a scholarship or not, to be her gift to God, her thank you for living as close to paradise as it was possible on this earth.

Jana recalled an afternoon when she had asked her mother about *her* quilts. She wondered if they had a "secret" like the Hawaiian ones did. Was it possible that her mother had more in common with the island ladies than she thought?

Her mother had opened her cedar chest and brought out a tissue-paper-wrapped bundle, placed it on the bed, and unwrapped it carefully, displaying a beautiful cover. "This is what we called a 'crazy quilt,' she told Jana, "They were very popular twenty years ago, all the rage. It's different sort of a memory quilt as well. You take pieces of clothing you wore on some memorable occasion and cut it into squares, they don't all need to be the same size, then piece them together and make a quilt. They're more for display than use. I made this when we lived in California. This was after we left Washington, where your father was stationed with the Army. Here is part of the skirt of the ball gown I wore to my first White House levee. I was so excited at the thought of meeting President and Mrs. Lincoln. And this was a gown I wore to attend a Military Ball." She pointed to triangles of peach satin embroidered with apricot suttachi.

Jana was intrigued, listening entranced as JoBeth talked and pointed out the different materials that had once been a dress or jacked or bodice, from which it had been cut and woven into this unique coverlet.

JoBeth started to refold the quilt, wrapping it carefully in tissue paper, then she pointed one slender finger to the patch of azure velvet. "See this, Jana, this piece of blue velvet? That was part of a dress I wore to the theater the night the president was murdered. I vowed I'd never wear it again. And I didn't. But I did cut it up and sewed it into the memory quilt. See, I bound it with black satin, those were the ribbons on my mourning bonnet, the one I wore to the Capitol Building where Lincoln lay in state —" JoBeth's eyes moistened and she shook her head. "It was such a sad time — still, I wanted to mark it as something very significant that happened in my life." Her hand moved over to some squares of jade taffeta. "And this was my wedding dress, Jana —"

"You didn't wear a white gown and veil, Mama?"

"No, darling, perhaps if we had married in my hometown. . . ." JoBeth looked pensive then she quickly brought out another quilt, spread it out so Jana could see it.

"This is my Friendship Quilt. I started it on our wagon train journey across the country and finished it when we got to California. You see, after the War, feelings still ran high between North and South, there was much bitterness and unforgiveness toward people still considered enemies on either side. Since your father had fought for the Union, we felt we could not return to the south to make our home, to build our life together. So we decided to come west. We joined a wagon train of thirty-five other families. It took us eight months and in those months I made many friends among the women. We all were boded by the excitement, the adventure of heading into an unknown place to start new lives. There were many hardships on the trail and so it was necessary and wonderful to have other women as friends, to support and help, to comfort you in case of sickness and yes, sometimes, in death." JoBeth paused, here eyes expressing some of the sorrowful memories. "See, this is a patchwork quilt, four squares to a patch and the center one has a special design. Each woman created her own patch to exchange with the others, embroidered her name, the date, where she was from, and where her family were headed." JoBeth held the quilt out so Jana could see.

"Millie Hartshorn, 1867, Bridgeville, Kentucky, Ho, for California." Jana read out loud. "Ruth Alice Webster, 1868, Dayton, Ohio, California." She looked at her mother. "How come they weren't all going to California like you and Papa?"

"There was what you call a turnoff point, those wagons going to Oregon went one way, the California group another. That's what makes this quilt so special. We knew when we exchanged our patches that we

161

might most likely never see each other again. But all I have to do is look at one of these autographed patches and that face comes right into mind. I can almost hear a certain laughter, a voice, a cheery word, remember a funny incident, or a sad one, or a time of sharing — I can never forget any of these ladies."

"Do you know where they are now? Do you ever hear from any of them?"

JoBeth shook her head. "No, none of us knew exactly where we'd be, or had an address where someone could write to us." She sighed. "That's the hard part, but, the good part is I'll always remember the happy times, where we were all young and looking forward to the future. Before anything bad happened to any of them or before any of us got old."

"I guess all quilts tell a story, don't they, Mama?"

"Yes, dear, I suppose they do," her mother replied.

And her mother could weave as fascinating a yarn about *her* quilts as any of the Hawaiian quilters could, Jana decided with satisfaction.

"How did you and Papa happen to come to Hawaii?" Jana asked.

"We hadn't planned that at all. But after

our little baby died, your brother Ross, name after *my* daddy, I was sad and not well for a long time. Your father thought a milder climate and change would be good for me. For both of us." She smiled at Jana, "And so it was. Not long after we went to Oahu we had *you!* So it was a happy move indeed." She put both hands on Jana's cheeks and kisser her. "See, 'all's well that ends well'."

Chapter 12

One early April afternoon, Jana was in the stationer's store shopping for art supplies. Busy examining a variety of brushes, she was startled to hear a familiar voice behind her.

"Well, if it isn't Miss Rutherford."

She turned around, brush in hand, and saw Bayard Preston. Completely taken by surprise, she exclaimed, "What are *you* doing here?"

"Home for spring vacation," he replied, regarding her with that look she had always found disconcerting.

"Did Edith come, too?" she asked hopefully.

Bayard shook his head. "No, she'll not be coming until June. She's spending her vacation in Newport, visiting one of her classmates. All sorts of parties and other exciting events were planned, and it proved too enticing to turn down for a mere trip home." His smile was slightly cynical. "My sister's become a social butterfly and also something of a belle. A few fellows you and I both know have been making weekend pilgrimages to Virginia to pay court to her." He paused. "Does that surprise you?"

"Not really," Jana said, but turned away so that her disappointment wouldn't be seen. Actually, it didn't surprise her. It was just what she'd been afraid would happen. Edith was growing away from Hawaii and her old friends. All in the space of less than a year. Jana continued to look through the display of brushes, saying casually, "That will be fun for her. But I'm sure your father will miss her."

"Father is on a business trip in Honolulu. I just returned from seeing him off in Hilo," Bayard said. "I'm to hold down the fort at the ranch for a few weeks." He added, "I hope you won't let me get too lonesome. How about going riding with me some morning?"

Jana took her time selecting two brushes before replying. She needed a moment to absorb the fact of the invitation. She remembered unpleasantly their last encounter. Turning around, she said coolly, "Mahalo, Bayard, but I'm very busy right now. I'm studying for final exams, and I've a painting project I'm working on that has to be finished by the first of the month."

Bayard raised a skeptical eyebrow. "It can't take *all* your time, surely? Besides, if you're working that hard, you deserve an hour or two off."

Jana moved to the next display and picked up a watercolor pad, opened it, and rubbed a page with her fingers to test its quality. Her experience with Bayard during the house party still rankled. She also resented the conversation she'd overheard between Bayard and the Colonel, the one that had persuaded Colonel Preston to send Edith away to school.

"I really don't think so, Bayard." Jana moved toward the cash register.

Bayard followed. "Come on, Jana, you know what they say about all work and no play," Bayard coaxed. "A ride? Take a picnic down to the valley?"

She remained unconvinced. "I don't think so."

While the clerk rang up Jana's purchases, Bayard stood beside her. After she had paid for them and received her change, he adroitly took the package.

"I'll carry these for you," he said ingratiatingly. "May I drive you home?"

"Mahalo, but no. I can walk."

"I *know* you can walk, Miss Rutherford," he teased. "I would be honored if you'd let me escort you home, either on foot or in my gig, which is just outside."

For some reason, Jana felt she would be more in control of this chance meeting if they walked. "It's only a short way," she said. "I can manage that, thank you." Jana put out her hand for her package.

Playfully he held it out of her reach. "No, you don't. Why are you being so independent, Miss Rutherford? Can't you tell I want to talk to you? Let me walk you home."

It would have seemed silly to continue to refuse or make a fuss, since Bayard seemed so determined. So she simply shrugged and they fell into step, walking together down the street. At the corner, they turned onto the road that led to the Rutherfords' house.

"What have you been doing with yourself since I last saw you?" Bayard asked.

"Studying mostly, painting," she replied. "Nothing very exciting. Tell me more about Edith."

"Oh, I don't keep track of all her doings. But I can tell you, there's not much studying going on at that fancy school. The most that the young ladies learn there is how to flirt, dance, and order from a French menu."

But that's exactly what you wanted for your sister, wasn't it? Jana was tempted to say. *Making good social contacts, mingling with people other than "just Hawaiians."*

"Evidently, Edith is at the top of her form, enjoying every minute. At least, that's what I gather by the amount of traffic that departs our campus on weekends," he laughed. "Quite a few keep the railroad tracks clacking between New Haven and Washington. I think Greg Amory is the most frequent traveler."

Aha, Jana thought, *so Edith is succeeding in achieving her goal.*

"Enough about my sister," Bayard said. "Tell me about yourself, Jana. What kind of plans are *you* making? What is this mysterious art project that you claim is taking up so much of your time that you can't go horseback riding?"

With some reluctance, but since she had given it as her excuse for having little free time, Jana told Bayard about her plan to try for an art scholarship.

By this time they had reached the Rutherfords' gate. Jana hesitated, wondering whether to ask Bayard to come in or not. While she debated, he glanced at their house. It was a gray and white Hawaiian-style bungalow built on stiltlike pillars, with a wraparound veranda. Surrounded by palms, lime trees, and banana trees, the yard was blooming with all sorts of flowering bushes.

"I've always loved Hawaiian cottages," Bayard said softly. "Their simplicity, their design — how they exactly fit right into the landscape. They're not an intrusion. I've often thought I'd like to be an architect. . . ." He gave a rueful smile. "However, of course, I'm destined to be a rancher." He sighed. "Aren't you going to invite me in, Jana? I've never been inside your house."

Embarrassed, Jana stammered, "Yes, please, do come in. I'm sure my mother would be happy to see you."

"Another time, maybe." He started to hand her the package but then held it just out of her reach and asked, "Will you think about going riding with me?"

Flustered by her lack of hospitality and eager to make amends, she impulsively answered, "Yes. I haven't ridden in quite a while. Since the Christmas before last, in fact, at the house party —" She broke off, wishing she hadn't brought it up.

Bayard looked thoughtful. "Ah yes, *that* Christmas. The house party. New Year's." He gave her a rueful glance. "As I remember, I wasn't in a very good mood for one reason or another. Did I somehow —" He halted, frowning. "We ended up rather badly, or am I mistaken?"

Jana put her hand on the gate latch, but

Bayard put his hand out so she could not lift it and asked, "Did I do or say anything to offend you? If so, I'm sorry. Please accept my apology?"

"It was nothing. I have to go in now."

"All right." He gave her the package. "May I come by sometime?"

"Of course." She pushed open the gate. "Mahalo, Bayard."

"My pleasure." He tipped his Panama hat. "My regards to your parents."

When Jana came into the house, her mother was in the kitchen, slicing *pumelos* to make marmalade.

"Who was that with you, dear? I didn't recognize him."

"Bayard Preston, Mama."

"Edith's brother?"

"I met him in town."

"Oh, is Edith home, too?"

"No, she won't be coming anytime soon. He says she quite loves it on the mainland."

"You will, too, dear, when you go."

Jana pursed her lips but did not answer. Instead, she left the kitchen and called back, "I think I'll go down to the beach for a while. I want to do some sketching."

In her room, Jana gathered up her paint box and a small tin cup for water, then unwrapped the package containing the new sketchbook and brushes, put them in her canvas bag. The encounter with Bayard had upset her somehow. It had stirred up something that still bothered her. She felt they had unfinished business between them. Seeing him again had brought it all back.

Down at the beach, she settled herself under a banyan tree and, backed by the dunes, propped her sketchbook against her knees, wiggling her bare toes in the warm sand. She always felt happier, calmer, near the ocean. Its vastness, its blue stretch to the horizon, seemed to make whatever was troubling her seem smaller, less important. She squeezed out some blue from the tube, dipped her brush into the water in her cup and stroked a horizontal line across the top of the page. She squinted out at the sea and saw that there were at least three shades of blue to be somehow captured and translated to her picture. How could she ever make it look as beautiful as she was seeing it, as it really was? She bent forward, moving her brush across the rough, textured sheet of paper.

Looking up again, she saw a surfer riding the crest of a wave, his bronzed body glistening in the sun. Immediately she was reminded of Kimo. How he must miss Hawaii, long for the sun-streaked skies, the curve of beach, the blue swells of the ocean. Did he miss her?

Did he have drifting dreams of the Big Island, its valleys, bamboo forests, the beach where they had walked so many times together? She thought of the sandcastles they had built as children, and her throat swelled and tightened. She closed her sketchbook, rested her chin on her knees, and watched as the surfer came ashore in a shower of foam, then turned and remounted his board and began paddling out past the swells again.

Kimo had been gone only a few months, and yet those days spent together on the beach, the days of childhood, and even the days of the Christmas before last when he had come home seemed a long time ago. They were fading even for her, who was trying to hold on to them. For Kimo, they may have disappeared entirely.

Chapter 13

School was closed for Easter vacation. Jana was sitting at her desk reviewing her notes for a book report when there was a light tap on her bedroom door and her mother's smiling face peered in. "Jana, Bayard Preston's here."

Jana frowned. What did *he* want? Probably just bored and lonely being at the ranch all by himself. With a sigh, she closed the book and got up. Passing her bureau mirror, she gave her hair a cursory pat. As she walked down the hall toward the porch, she heard her mother's voice and Bayard's deeper one. She hesitated a moment before joining them, determined to be cool, to not be taken in by his charm. Jana opened the screen door, walked out, and deliberately used the Hawaiian greeting. "Aloha."

Bayard rose from the wicker chair. He looked crisp and handsome in a beige linen suit, polished boots, white shirt.

"Hello, Jana. I was just telling your mother I have to drive over to Kamuela and would love to have your company. We could have lunch at the hotel. Will you come?"

Her mother smiled encouragingly. Jana could see that Bayard had already convinced *her* that it would be a good idea. His look challenged, as if he suspected she was trying to think of an excuse.

"Why not, dear? It would be a nice break," her mother suggested mildly. To Bayard she said, "Jana's been working very hard, getting ready for exams and finishing her painting projects."

"Then, an outing should be just what she needs," Bayard said.

"I have a book report to write . . . ," Jana started to say, but that sounded indecisive and Bayard took the initiative.

"Do come, Jana. It will do you good."

"Yes, dear, why don't you?" urged her mother.

Caught between the two, she could think of no reasonable excuse. Nothing that wouldn't sound rude. So she gave in and went to put on a fresh blouse and get her straw sailor hat.

Within minutes she found herself in his surrey, with his high-stepping horse trotting along the beach road toward Kamuela. Glancing over at Bayard's handsome profile, Jana wondered again at the invitation. He was probably bored and at loose ends up at the ranch alone. She felt the same ambiguity about him she had felt at the Christmas house party. In the year since then, she had come to the conclusion that Bayard Preston was attractive but dangerous. She still thought so. Yet she had not forgotten how she had felt when he kissed her.

It was a perfect Hawaiian day. Cloudless blue skies, balmy breezes stirring the fringe of the surrey's canvas top. All along the road, flowers of every kind and description were in bloom. Hibiscus, ginger, plumeria, and the feathery blossoms of the jacaranda trees scented the air with perfume.

It was only a short drive to Kamuela, and they were soon in the center of the small town.

"I have to stop at the bank, sign some business papers for my father. Do you mind waiting? It won't take long, and then we'll have lunch."

"Not at all," she replied as Bayard pulled the surrey into a shady spot across the street from the bank.

As she sat waiting, Jana tried to remember why she resented Bayard so much. It wasn't that last angry confrontation in the Preston garden on New Year's Day. At last she realized what it was. She still blamed him for Edith's going away to finishing school. His urging his father to send her had really been a result of his own frustration, his ambiguity about his bicultural background.

Before she had thoroughly thought it through again, Bayard was back and they drove over to the oceanfront hotel. At the entrance, a hotel employee helped them from the surrey, then led the horse away. Bayard placed his hand under Jana's elbow, and together they went up the wide steps to the veranda. Here white rush-bottom rocking chairs lined the long porch, and varicolored hibiscus trailed from baskets hung along the fretwork.

Although she had often admired the stately dignity of the impressive, white-pillared structure, Jana had never been inside. The Rutherfords did not move in the same kind of circles as the Prestons and never dined out. At the entrance to the dining room, the waiter greeted Bayard by name and suggested they take a table on the screened porch.

"Would you enjoy that?" Bayard asked.

A little overawed by the luxurious setting, Jana simply nodded. They were led out to a screened-in area overlooking a terraced garden of palms and winding paths among brilliant flower beds. A cooling breeze wafted gently in from the ocean. The waiter seated Jana, pulling out a white wicker chair and handing her a large menu, then quietly departed to a discreet distance to await their order.

The tablecloth and napkins were pale pink linen, and the water glasses sparkled like crystal. Jana noticed fashionably dressed men and women at the other tables. This was a part of island life she had rarely seen at close hand: people of wealth and leisure who lunched expensively at this exclusive place as a matter of course. Bayard, perfectly at ease and assured, was studying the menu.

So many choices were confusing, so Jana let Bayard order. After bringing them iced tea with mint sprigs and slices of lemon, the waiter went away. Jana began to relax and enjoy this new experience. She took a sip of her tea and murmured, "The view is lovely."

"So is *mine,*" Bayard said, regarding her with amused eyes.

She ignored the flattery, discounting it as automatic — he'd had lots of social practice at that sort of remark. Deciding that his sister might be a safer topic of conversation, Jana asked, "So exactly when *will* Edith be coming home?"

Bayard shrugged. "When she gets bored with Newport, I suppose. As you may have noticed, my sister has a short attention span. But to answer your question, more than likely Father will insist she come back with him in a few weeks, and she'll probably bring some of her friends." He pulled a grimace. "A bunch of sillies, if I've ever seen any. All giggles, flirting, game playing!" He rolled his eyes. "Deliver me. Not an intelligent statement in any of them."

"Ah, but isn't *that* what *you* wanted Edith exposed to?" Jana demanded, feeling a bit of spiteful pleasure in turning the tables on him. "If I'm not mistaken, you said, 'Edith needs to be with other kinds of people, not just *Hawaiians.*' "

Bayard frowned. "Now that I think about it, I admit I did say that — *think* that. I'd forgotten," he admitted. "And that was before I'd met any of the young ladies at Millvale Hall!" He paused, then leaned his folded arms on the table. "I'd forgotten how refreshing it is to be with someone like you, Jana. Someone who's forthright, natural, not afraid to have her own opinions."

"Then, you've changed your mind about *independent* women?"

His frown deepened. "Is that something else I said that you're quoting? Aha, I must have said something that really offended you, or you wouldn't be bringing up this. Did I?"

The waiter arrived with their order, so she did not have to answer Bayard's question. Perhaps it was all best forgotten anyhow.

Jana realized she was very hungry, and she picked up her fork and began to eat shrimp salad served in a melon shell garnished with pineapple spears and kiwi fruit. But Bayard leaned toward her. "You didn't answer. So if I did hurt your feelings or anything, I'm very sorry."

"It's all right, Bayard. It doesn't matter. I think I'm too sensitive sometimes."

"Then I did. Just say you forgive me. You're the last person I'd ever want to hurt."

"Yes, it's all right. I'm sure you have better things to think about than me."

"You're wrong, Jana. I've had a lot of time to think about it. About you." He lowered his voice. "When I saw you that Christmas, it was the first time since you were a little girl. Or at least it was the first time I'd *really* noticed you. I recognized something in you. I didn't know what it was that drew me, but I felt we had a bond I hadn't realized before. It's very strong, very powerful."

"And that is?"

"Hawaii."

She looked surprised.

"Down deep I have the same feeling you have. Born here but still a *haole*. It causes a kind of dual personality." Bayard gave a self-deprecating little laugh. "Not that I'm one of those new scientific fellows that talk about childhood influences on the adult character. Most of that, I think, is a lot of rubbish. But Father sending me to the mainland at an impressionable age *did* have an effect on me. I felt caught between two worlds, actually. He did what he thought was best. Wanted me to get the kind of education he didn't think was possible here on the island. For *me,* at least. Then I went on to Yale, still trapped in this dichotomy —" He halted suddenly. "I don't know why I'm rattling on like this. I must be boring you to death."

"No, you're not. It's very interesting —"

"You're sure?"

Jana did not have a chance to respond to Bayard's question, because the waiter came to check if everything was all right and if they wanted dessert.

At the same time, four gentlemen wearing white linen suits and Panama hats came out onto the porch and took seats at a table nearby. One of them, seeing Bayard, waved and then excused himself from his friends and came over to their table. Bayard introduced Jana, and the two men spoke for a few minutes about a business matter the man was arranging for Colonel Preston. When he left, Bayard and Jana did not pick up the thread of their conversation again. Jana was relieved. It was edging on too personal a tone.

Finished, they rose, and after Bayard had signed for the bill to be put on his father's account, they left. Back in the surrey, on their way to Waimea, Bayard gave Jana a sidelong glance. "You're not sorry you came, are you?"

"No, not really." Thinking that might have sounded ambivalent, she added, "It was very nice of you to suggest it, to think of me."

"I think about you a great deal, Jana. More often than you'd guess."

Again she felt that this was leading to an exchange that might prove to be too personal, so she skirted around the subject, remarking on some particularly lovely anthuriums. "Oh look, I'd love to try to paint those."

When they reached the Rutherfords' cottage, he helped her down from the surrey, "When may I see you again? Tomorrow?"

She shook her head. "Tomorrow's

Sunday. I go to church and Sunday is our family day. I usually take Nathan to the beach, or we visit some of my parents' friends."

Bayard looked disappointed. "You said you might like to go riding? Remember?"

Jana hesitated. She wasn't sure seeing Bayard again was a good idea.

However, he persisted as he walked her to the gate. "I'll come by sometime in the middle of the week. We can make plans then. All right?"

"Mahalo," she said, again deliberately using the Hawaiian word. She didn't know exactly why, but it was almost as if she were testing Bayard.

"And you will think about going riding?"

"Yes."

"Good." He seemed satisfied. Bayard Preston was used to getting his own way. He turned and went whistling back to his surrey. Jana went into the house.

Her mother lifted her head from her sewing and looked at her daughter with thoughtful eyes. "Did you have a nice time, dear?"

"Yes, it was lovely. Lunch was delicious."

"Bayard is a handsome young man, isn't he? And a perfect gentleman. You can certainly tell he has been educated on the mainland."

"He says Edith won't be home for another month," Jana told her. "Bayard says Colonel Preston has gone to the mainland and they'll return together. She's visiting some school friends in Newport, Rhode Island."

"Newport?" her mother repeated. "That's a very fashionable resort for very wealthy people. Edith must be traveling with high society."

Jana darted a quick look at her mother. Was there a tinge of regret in her voice? Jana knew that her mother had come from a fine old southern family. She had left it all to follow her idealistic husband west — to California first, then to Hawaii. She had probably had all the luxuries and refinements of a gentle upbringing in an affluent home. Did she miss it? Did she want that kind of life for her daughter?

Jana did not realize *she* was the object of her mother's thoughtful speculation. Looking at Jana as she filled a glass of water from the cast-iron kitchen pump, JoBeth Rutherford thought about what a graceful, attractive young woman Jana was becoming. What exactly did the future hold for her here on the island? What did she hope for her daughter? Of course she wanted her to find love and happiness. But was it wrong to hope she would have a life easier than her own had been? She recalled her rather practical Aunt Jo Cady saying, "A woman can fall in love as easily with a wealthy man as a poor one." But was that true? It was for Aunt Cady, evidently — Uncle Madison had been a prosperous lawyer. JoBeth herself had given no thought at all as to whether Wes was rich or poor. It hadn't mattered. She had loved him with all her heart, and they had — in spite of everything — been happy.

But what about Jana? JoBeth felt sometimes that her daughter was a hopeless dreamer, impractical, romantic, given to fantasy. What would life hold for someone like her?

With a man like Bayard Preston, Jana would never lack anything. She'd have a beautiful home, clothes, every luxury, travel . . . the things a talented person like Jana would enjoy. There would be no financial worries, no scraping or scrimping.

Was Edith's older brother becoming romantically interested in Jana? The question lingered tantalizingly.

Chapter 14

On the Saturday before Easter, Jana assembled all the necessary implements to help Nathan dye three dozen eggs for the Easter party the Rutherfords held every year. They had hard-boiled them the evening before and let them cool overnight.

"Now's the fun part!" the little boy said eagerly as he watched Jana spread newspaper on the kitchen table, place the bowls filled with food coloring in a row of red, blue, yellow, and green.

"That's right," she smiled, getting out two big spoons for them to use for dipping the eggs. She had also brought her paint box and brushes and a glass jar of water, to add designs and finishing touches when the colored eggs were dry.

"The next fun part will be hiding them, won't it, Jana?"

"Yes, and Papa has promised to help so *you* won't know where all the eggs are and get them all and fill your basket before anyone else!" she laughed, tousling her little brother's hair.

"That wouldn't be fair," he declared, but his eyes sparkled and his grin was mischievous.

"No, it wouldn't."

The process of dyeing took both of them over an hour, and Nathan soon tired of the tedious job.

"When do we get to paint on flowers and stuff?" he asked Jana.

"I guess you could start on some of the first ones we did. They should be dry by now." Jana tested the first half dozen with one finger. Satisfied that they were ready for the additional decoration, she got Nathan set up at one end of the table, then sat down beside him to get him started. She was painting some daisies on the shell of one, when Nathan suddenly flung down his brush in frustration, spattering paint.

"Mine are awful, Jana! Next to yours, they look terrible!"

"No, they don't! Not at all. Here, let me show you. You're doing just fine. You have to be patient, that's all."

"But yours are so much prettier. That's because you're an artist. Everyone says so."

"Well, maybe. I guess so, but *yours* are special, because *you* are doing them yourself. Mine are different, not better," she consoled him.

"Did you always know you were an artist, Jana? Even when you were little — my age?"

"I always liked to draw and paint," she replied.

"So you did know you wanted to be an artist when you grew up?"

"I guess so."

"I know what I'm going to be when *I* grow up," Nathan said firmly.

"What's that? A teacher like Papa?"

He shook his head vigorously. "No! A builder and woodworker like Kimo."

Surprised, Jana looked at him. "Like Kimo?"

"Yes. I miss Kimo. When is he coming back?"

"I'm not sure," Jana answered, thinking about how long Kimo had been gone and how long it had been since she'd heard from him. "Soon, I hope."

"I love Kimo," Nathan said matter-of-factly.

Jana gave him a hug, saying to herself, *I do, too.*

Easter morning dawned brilliant with sunshine, the air sweetly fragrant with flowers and filled with the sound of church bells. Jana had a new bonnet, a new blouse, and a new prayer book. After an early breakfast and while her mother went to get dressed, Jana got Nathan buttoned into a white sailor suit. It was rather stiff and he squirmed uncomfortably, making the job almost impossible. However, in the end, with his curls slicked down and a blue silk scarf tied neatly, he looked almost cherubic. Then the whole family walked the short distance to the small church where they worshiped.

It had dozens of twins all over the island, with the same tiny porch, peaked roof, and bell tower. Pink anthuriums bloomed on either side of the steps leading inside, and cala lilies were clustered in profusion on the altar. The Rutherfords settled into their regular pew just as the choir marched in to the chords of the small organ. The congregation rose to its feet, joining in the opening hymn, which was first sung in Hawaiian, then in English.

"Holy, holy, holy, Lord God Almighty, heaven and earth are filled with your glory. Hosanna in the highest. Blessed is he of Israel who comes in the name of the Lord."

The voices lifted up, mellow and clear, and enveloped Jana in a lovely peace. The beautiful words swept her up into their meaning. *In whatever language the praise is sung,* she thought, *it must be a sweet sound in the Lord's ear. All over the world, in all different tongues, believers are greeting the risen Savior, King of Kings, Lord of Lords.*

Jana lowered her head so no one could see the tears that sprang spontaneously into her eyes.

The joyous service concluded with Communion and then a final hymn. The choir filed out, and the congregation followed them outside into the lovely morning, greeting each other with traditional hugs and kisses, saying, *"Ka la i ala hou ai ka Haku."*

To her astonishment, Jana saw Bayard standing in the churchyard. Dressed in a spotless white linen suit, ruffled shirt, and Panama hat, he came toward her.

"Good morning and happy Easter," he said, bowing slightly. His gaze moved over her admiringly. "That is one of the prettiest bonnets I've yet seen, and the lady wearing it is quite charming as well."

"What in the world are you doing here?" she asked.

Bayard placed one hand on his heart, with an injured look. "Don't tell me you suspected I was one of those Christmas and Easter Christians?" he demanded. Then, with an ironic smile, he added, "Which, unfortunately, I am. If I reform, will you forgive me?"

"You don't need to ask *my* forgiveness. I shouldn't have —" She broke off, embarrassed that he had surmised the truth. She *had* been surprised — in fact, astonished — to see him at church.

"Not at all. You're right."

"Whether you're a churchgoer or not is none of my business."

"I'd like you to make it your business," Bayard said in a low voice. "I can't imagine anything more pleasant than being reformed by you."

Jana blushed and was glad to be rescued when her parents and Nathan joined them. Bayard greeted them all graciously. To Jana's surprise, her mother said, "We're having an Easter breakfast party and an old-fashioned Easter egg hunt for the children, Bayard. You'd be more than welcome if you cared to join the fun."

"I'd be delighted," he accepted at once.

As they fell into step behind her parents, Jana could not resist saying, "I didn't know you went in for such things."

"Maybe there's a lot you don't know about me, Jana. If you'd give me a chance, I'd reveal some hidden qualities you may not even suspect." His tone was light but his eyes were serious.

"I'm intrigued," Jana murmured, but she was not sure she wanted a chance to get to know Bayard Preston better. It was like looking down a road that had danger signs all along the way, with a sharp curve in the distance so that you could not see where it ended.

There was no more time for Jana and Bayard to be alone. Friends had already begun to gather at the Rutherfords' for this annual event. Jana had to help her mother set out the fruit and banana nut breads, keep the adults' coffee cups filled, and pour pineapple juice. When the children began clamoring to begin the egg hunt, Bayard shed his jacket and enthusiastically joined Mr. Rutherford in supervising. Bayard seemed to have great fun running around with the children, pointing out hiding places to some of the smaller, slower ones.

At last all the eggs were discovered, and families with children, their baskets full of eggs and candy, began to leave.

Bayard retrieved his coat, said his thanks and good-byes to the Rutherfords, then found Jana.

"Will you come riding with me to-morrow?" he asked as she walked with him to the gate. "Remember what I said earlier? There's no telling how much I might improve if we spend enough time together."

"Oh Bayard, I'm not sure. . . ."

"There's no school, so you have no excuse. I'll come for you at nine. You can ride Palani. She's a gentle, copper-colored mare with a sensitive mouth. You'll love her. I guarantee it."

Chapter 15

True to his word, Bayard came by for Jana at nine the following morning, and they rode up to the ranch in a small, open buggy. At the Preston stables, one of the grooms brought out the horse Bayard had promised her, a lovely little mare with delicate legs, shining coat, and blond mane. Bayard patted her nose, murmuring something, then turned to Jana, smiling. "See, isn't she a beauty? You'll find her a dream to ride."

He checked the saddle. Then as the groom stood at Palani's head, Bayard helped Jana to mount. As he had promised, Palani was sweet tempered, with an easy mouth. As soon as Jana picked up the reins, she felt an instant response from the horse.

"Where's yours?" she asked.

"Come along, I'll show you," Bayard said. He took the tooled leather saddle and tack that the groom handed him. With long strides, he went past the corral and into the pasture. Jana, on horseback, followed at a walk.

At the pasture, Bayard whistled through his fingers, and a horse that had been grazing on the hilltop lifted its head, ears pricked up, and whinnied. Then, with a toss of its head, silver mane flying, the mixed gray horse galloped across the field. Approaching Bayard, he slowed to a kind of prancing trot, circled Bayard a couple of times, then stopped, one hoof pawing the ground.

Bayard ran his hand along the horse's back, stroking it gently, then leaned for a moment against its arched neck. Slowly he slipped the bridle over the horse's bowed head, adjusted the bit, then saddled him. Swinging lightly into the saddle, he came over to where Jana was halted on her mare, watching. Grinning, he said, "A paniolo at heart." He leaned forward in his saddle toward her. "If I'd been in the New Year's rodeo, would you have accepted *my* talisman?"

Taken aback, she countered, "Why *didn't* you ride that day?"

He shrugged. "Who knows? Maybe I was inhibited by my guests. Those *haoles*, strangers to our land and our customs, think we're wild enough. I didn't want to give them any more ammunition." He whirled his horse around, shouting over his shoulder, "Come on, let's go!"

He galloped off. Jana loosened her reins, and Palani followed in an easy canter. It was a glorious morning and an exhilarating ride. Bayard always kept a few lengths ahead of Jana, but she didn't care. She was not in competition with him, as Edith might have been. She was enjoying the rocking motion of Palani's gait, and the feeling of freedom engendered by the wind in her face, tugging her hat back, blowing her loosened hair. She had missed riding as she and Edith had often done, traveling over these hills together. Jana suddenly realized how much she missed Edith as well.

However, there wasn't time to indulge in nostalgia about the old days of comradeship, for Bayard had reached the top of the cliff and had halted there. As she came alongside and reined, she saw what Bayard was looking at: the rolling green hillside and, in the distance, the ocean, stripes of varied blue stretching out to a cloudless horizon. For a few minutes neither spoke as they absorbed the breathtaking view. Finally he said quietly, "Shall we go home now? Next time we'll ride down to the valley."

Next time? Jana thought. Bayard was assuming there would be a next time. She watched him turn his horse and start back toward the ranch. Following him at a slower pace, Jana recalled vividly her last ride down the precipitous, almost perpendicular path to the legendary Valley of the Kings. Gradually she caught up to him, and with both horses slowed to an easy canter, they rode back to the ranch.

At the stables, Bayard quickly dismounted, came around to Jana's side, held up his arms to help her down from her saddle. She stood for a minute smoothing Palani's mane, rubbing her nose, murmuring affectionate thanks for the lovely ride. Watching her, Bayard said, "She could be yours, you know. You two are kindred spirits."

Startled, Jana looked at him. She was not quite sure what he meant, but she did not dare ask. Bayard continued to confuse and bewilder her.

One of the grooms led the horses away to be rubbed down and fed, and Bayard and Jana walked up to the house.

"One day we should ride to the volcano side of the island. Would you like that?" he said.

"I don't know about that," she answered slowly. Hawaii still had two active volcanoes, Mauna Kea and Kilauea. Jana had been into the volcano country on the other side of the island. She had found it oppressive and forbidding, and when you got close, the smell of sulfur fumes was heavy. She knew all about the ancient beliefs regarding Pele, the goddess of fire, who was supposed to dwell within the volcano. In the olden days, native people tried to appease her with all sorts of gifts so that her anger would not erupt and send fiery molten lava flowing over their land, their homes, their crops.

"Well, you *will* go riding with me again, won't you?" Bayard asked.

"Yes, of course. And thank you for allowing me to ride Palani. She was wonderful."

They had reached the house, but before going inside, Bayard stopped and reached for Jana's hand, held it, and said, "I meant what I said back there. She could be yours."

Jana looked at him, puzzled. Before she had time to answer, Meipala came out onto the veranda.

"Mr. Bayard, there's a gentleman here to see you. A Mr. Pollard from the bank. He says he has a message from the Colonel."

Bayard frowned, then said to Jana, "This shouldn't take long. Probably more papers to sign. I have Father's power of attorney. You can sit out here on the porch. Meipala will bring you something cool to drink." He excused himself and went into the house.

A few minutes later Meipala brought Jana a glass of cool guava juice. As she handed her the tall glass, Meipala asked, "You hear from Edith?"

Jana shook her head. "Not much. She's not much of a letter writer. From what Bayard says, she's having a really good time."

"Too good, if you ask me," Meipala sniffed. "Did he tell you she bringing party of girls with her when she come home?"

"He mentioned something about it."

Then Meipala asked Jana about her family and her own studies.

"Akela and I will graduate in June. But we miss Kiki — we always thought we three would finish school together."

"You *should* have. Don't know what got into the Colonel to send her so far away." Meipala shook her head sorrowfully. "I thought she would miss the island more than she seems to."

Just then Bayard came out onto the porch, accompanied by Mr. Pollard, so they had no more time to discuss Edith. Mr. Pollard recognized Jana, whom he had met at the

Kamuela Hotel when she was there with Bayard, and greeted her cordially. Then he said to Bayard, "Well, I suppose that's all for now. If you want to go over this further or discuss it later, I'm always available."

"Fine, sir." Bayard's voice seemed unusually crisp.

He walked Mr. Pollard to his buggy and saw him off. When he came back to join Jana, Bayard seemed preoccupied. She hoped the banker had not brought worrying news. However, his good humor returned at Meipala's suggestion that she have their lunch served out there on the veranda. She poured him a glass of guava juice, then left them.

Jana leaned back against the striped linen pillows of the white wicker rocking chair. She felt pleasantly tired from their ride and completely relaxed and comfortable. What a heavenly day, she thought. And how delicious it felt to just lazily rock and stare out at the lush gardens and the distant blue ribbon of the ocean. She didn't even feel the least bit guilty. At home, nobody ever sat around just doing nothing! This was pure luxury.

And to think that this was how the Prestons and their friends spent their days. They took this kind of leisurely life for granted. Doing whatever occurred to them — no chores, no duties, no time frame, people to wait on them . . .

Her dreamy thoughts were interrupted by the arrival of one of the uniformed Chinese house servants. He carried a large tray from which he set a low, round table with their lunch: a delicious assortment of fruit, small, hot shrimp-filled pastries, salad, a loaf of banana nut bread, and a pitcher of iced tea.

"I could soon be spoiled here," Jana remarked half jokingly as she helped herself to the appetizing array of food.

"And why not? It's good to see things appreciated and enjoyed. Isn't that what all this is for? To be enjoyed?"

"I don't know whether my father would agree with you, Bayard!" she laughed.

"Does he frown on people enjoying themselves?"

"Oh no, not that. But he does believe there is more purpose to life than just enjoying oneself. You know: life is real, life is earnest."

"That's a throwback to the early missionary days. They disapproved of almost everything about Hawaiian life and tried to change it." Bayard paused. "However, it worked in the reverse. The Hawaiians converted them to an easier way of life, a more relaxed style of living. That's what makes this island so special." He halted abruptly. "It seems we had this sort of conversation once before, and we ended up — how was it?"

"I think I just misunderstood, Bayard. I thought — well, that you were somehow ashamed of loving Hawaii."

"No, it wasn't that. It's just that I can't be completely Hawaiian. . . . I'm sort of torn in two. Maybe when I come back here to live for good, take over the running of the ranch . . . Maybe then it will seem more —" He broke off. "I guess I'm talking a lot of rubbish."

"Not at all. Kiki and I argue about which one of us is more Hawaiian than the other. At least, we used to. . . ." Jana's voice trailed off uncertainly. She wasn't sure what Kiki thought anymore.

"Of course, her mother *was* Hawaiian."

"Yes, but I was *born* in Honolulu — she was born in San Francisco."

"I was born here on the island," Bayard said. "That makes *us* technically natives, doesn't it? And give us a special relationship." He gazed at her thoughtfully. "Wouldn't you say?"

For some reason, Jana felt a little tingling sensation. Somehow she couldn't pull her own gaze away from Bayard's. Her heart fluttered erratically. Her hand holding the iced tea glass shook, and her fingers slipped on its frosty surface. She put it down quickly, afraid she might drop it. She wiped her mouth with the napkin and said, "I really think I'd better be going, Bayard. I've been gone all morning, and I promised Nathan I'd take him to the beach this afternoon." She brushed the crumbs from her lap, folded her napkin and placed it beside her empty plate on the tray, and rose.

"Must you go?" he asked, but he got to his feet also.

"Yes, I really must."

Bayard was quiet as he drove Jana home in the surrey. A thoughtful air had replaced his earlier lighthearted manner. Jana wondered again whether it was something Mr. Pollard had said. Or was it something in their own conversation that was bothering him? At the gate of her house, he said, "Mahalo, Jana, for making it such a pleasant time. Remember, you promised to go riding with me again. Palani will be disappointed if you don't."

"School starts again next week," she reminded him, feeling a little twinge of regret that she wouldn't be free to go on the kind of spontaneous expedition Bayard had suggested.

"Ah, that's right. You're still a schoolgirl, aren't you?" His eyes were teasing. "Well, we'd better make the most of this week, then, hadn't we?"

She watched Bayard's buggy, the fringe on its striped canopy swinging jauntily, disappear down the road. It had been fun today. More fun than she had ever anticipated having with Edith's older brother. She had been comfortable and at ease with him. No, not exactly that. Underneath, there had been a tiny bit of tension. As though she were on the brink of something. Something in the way Bayard looked at her, treated her, that was different from last Christmas. Something that was both exciting and a little frightening. . . .

That night, lying in bed and looking out her window at the shadow of the palm tree against the star-studded sky, Jana let her mind wander. . . . What would it be like to have the kind of life the Prestons had, a life of leisure and luxury and servants and trips and never worrying about money or what other people said or thought about you? What would that really be like?

She had never before really envied Edith Preston, had never thought much about what a contrast their families and lives were. Actually, it was Akela's family, the ohana, that Jana had looked at longingly. Now, however, there was a certain allure in the idea of being wealthy, free from worries about the future or about getting a scholarship. Edith had no such thoughts. She would always be taken care of. There would always be money for whatever she wanted to do, wherever she wanted to go. . . .

What was it Bayard had said? First about Palani — "She could be yours." Had he just meant she had ridden the gentle horse well and the mare had responded well to her? Or had he meant more than that? Had he meant it literally?

Then when he had looked at her and said, "We have a special bond, a special relationship, don't we?" They were both islanders. Born here but still of white parentage. It did give one pause. It did make one think.

Her eyelids felt heavy. It had been a long day, an interesting day, a day that in some ways seemed a turning point.

She was getting too sleepy to think it through, but as she drifted off, it was of Bayard Preston she was thinking. . . .

Chapter 16

School started again, and at first Jana found it hard to settle back down to the routine of studies and homework. The interlude of impromptu outings with Bayard had set her off track. It had been an interesting time but one that was also rather disturbing. Her long-held view of Bayard had altered, and yet she still wasn't sure she really knew or understood him.

One afternoon a few days after classes had resumed, Jana accompanied Akela into town on an errand for Tutu. Akela was to pick up some spools of thread that Tutu had ordered. Just as they came out of the fabric store, they practically ran into Bayard, who was coming down the street. Jana was surprised to be so glad to see him.

Bayard seemed equally surprised but pleased. "Well hello, ladies. Would you give me the pleasure of taking you somewhere for a cool drink?"

"Mahalo, Bayard," Akela said. "I'm sorry,

I can't. I have to hurry home. Tutu's working on one of her quilts and needs these." She held up the small bag containing the thread.

"Another time, then. How about you, Jana? You're not in any hurry, are you?"

"No." Jana turned to Akela. "Do you mind?"

"Of course not. You two go ahead," Akela smiled. "Have a nice time."

"Do give my regards to your grandmother, won't you?" Bayard called after her, then held out his arm to Jana. "Come along, then."

Jana slipped her hand through his arm, and they walked down the street to a nearby confectionery store.

"Limeade?" he asked when they went inside.

"Lovely."

Bayard placed their order at the counter. He received two tall, frosted glasses and suggested, "Let's take these outside."

They went to one of the umbrellaed tables on the small lanai and sat down.

"You've changed my luck today," he told her.

"How's that?"

"Oh, I've just come from a long, boring session at the bank. My father's business.

But while he's gone, I have to take care of some things. I was feeling very dull when I left there, and then — lo and behold!" He threw out his hand dramatically. "There you were! What a treat!"

Jana laughed at his foolishness but felt pleased. She held up her glass in a toasting gesture. "But it's I who's getting the treat."

"You'll have to pay for it, though," Bayard smiled. "I need you to help me select a gift for someone. A lady. Now, don't get any ideas. It's a hostess gift. For Mrs. Amory. You remember Greg, don't you? Well, I've spent several weekends with them over the last year or so, and I want to send her something special. But I don't know what, and I need your artist's eye to help me find something."

"Any idea what she might like?"

"I think something distinctly Hawaiian." He pulled a face. "You know how mainlanders are. They think anything from the islands is *exotic*."

"Well, that shouldn't be difficult. There's a wonderful shop not far from here that has beautiful things."

"Great. As soon as we finish here, let's go and take a look."

The store was one Jana had often lingered outside of, gazing raptly into the display windows at the merchandise. She had never ventured inside, because she knew that the prices were way beyond anything she could ever afford. It was even more marvelous than she had imagined. She wandered about, admiring the delicate porcelain vases, the intricate jade sculptures, the exquisite embroidered silk screens, the jewelry.

"Do you see anything that appeals to you?" Bayard asked.

Jana widened her eyes. "Of course! Half the store!" she answered in a hushed voice. Then, smiling, she led him over to a display of blue-and-white china and pointed to two graceful candleholders and a matching bowl.

"Yes, I think I agree with you," Bayard nodded. "I believe that would suit Mrs. Amory's taste very well." He gave Jana an approving grin. "You're a genius."

While his gift was being boxed and wrapped, they waited at the large jewelry display counter. Pearls and jade in all shades, shapes, and styles — rings, necklaces, earrings, pins, and pendants — were set out on dark velvet. Jana was totally entranced.

"Something here you'd like?" Bayard asked quietly.

"I've always loved pearls. They have such a quality of surprise about them. How they're found even seems romantic — out of the sea, like some lovely gift."

"I'd like to get you something. Pick something out."

Startled, Jana looked at him, stepping back from the display case. "Oh, I couldn't, Bayard. It wouldn't be — be proper."

"Why not? Just as a little thank-you for helping me today."

"That's not necessary, Bayard," she protested. "I enjoyed doing it. You don't owe me anything."

"What if I just want to do it? What's wrong with that?" His mouth twisted sarcastically. "Is it some kapu I never heard of?"

A *kapu* was an ancient rule of the Hawaiian culture, existing long before the white man came to the islands. There had been placed upon the people many restrictions that had to be obeyed. Certain things were forbidden. These included eating certain types of fish, which were reserved for royalty, or passing within the shadow of a king or his possessions.

A kapu breaker was severely punished. It was believed that if he or she went unpunished, some disaster, perhaps a *tsunami* — a tidal wave — or a volcanic eruption, might occur. However, if the culprit managed to reach a place designated as a refuge, the person was safe. All who sought entry there were admitted — vanquished warriors and noncombatants as well. It was a sanctuary in which offenders could stay as long as they wanted, but if they left, they were again subject to punishment. One such place, on the south Kona coast, was called City of Refuge.

Jana bristled slightly at his tone. She didn't like hearing jokes about the Old Hawaiian culture. She felt that it should be respected, not ridiculed. "No, of course not. It's just that . . . a young lady should not accept an expensive piece of jewelry from a gentleman unless they are —" She stopped short.

Bayard smiled as he finished her sentence. "You mean, unless they are engaged?"

Jana's cheeks flamed. "Well, yes."

"Wouldn't allowance be made if it was something quite small, given in friendship?" Bayard persisted. "For instance . . ." He leaned forward and pointed down into the display case, to a small brooch, a pale pink, fan-shaped shell in which a tiny pink pearl nestled. It was a delicate piece of jewelry, and Jana would have loved it. Still, it was out of the question. Her mother would have a fit! Reluctantly she shook her head.

"Mahalo, Bayard — it was a very nice thought, but no."

Just then the clerk returned with Bayard's package. Bayard peeled off several bills in payment and they left the shop.

"Could I talk you into going for a horse-back ride along the beach this evening?" he asked.

"Oh, you certainly know how to tempt a girl!" she laughed. "I have a history test tomorrow. I have to really study hard tonight."

Bayard gave her a long, steady look.

"I never met a girl so honest or one with so much character."

Again Jana felt her face grow warm. When she was with Bayard, he often said things that made her react strongly.

For a moment a kind of uneasy silence tingled between them.

"Well, I have to go, Bayard," Jana said and took a few steps away from him.

"Could I give you a ride? My surrey is right across the park."

"No, thanks. I'll walk."

All the way home Jana thought about the afternoon, the time she had just spent with Bayard, and how much she would have liked the small shell pin with the tiny pearl.

Chapter 17

During the next two weeks, there were other impromptu meetings, other little excursions, other unplanned outings, with Bayard. He would often show up with Palani on a lead and insist that Jana put aside her books and go riding.

It was getting near the end of school, and there were final exams and several special activities for the graduates. An open house was planned to which the island superintendent of secondary schools, magistrates, and other dignitaries had been invited. The seniors had been asked to bring samples of their artistic work or crafts to exhibit. The small island high school wanted to show off its students and their accomplishments.

Late one afternoon when Jana was going through her portfolio, trying to pick out some of her watercolors for the school exhibit, Bayard stopped by. She had spread some of her watercolors on the living room floor to look at them and decide which ones to submit. When she saw him standing out-side the screen door, she called, "Come in, Bayard. Maybe you can help me decide."

He took off his boots and came in on stocking-clad feet. Jana, barefooted, was stepping between the pictures, moving them around for better viewing, selectively dis-carding some, leaving others. Bayard stood beside her. "You're very good, Jana," he said as he examined her work carefully. "I had no idea."

"Mahalo," she said rather absently. "I'm not so sure. These are not as good as I'd like them to be." She shook her head. "I've ne-glected my watercolors the last few months. I spent so much time working on the design I submitted for a scholarship to art school."

"You haven't heard yet, then? From the art school?"

"No, and I'm kind of losing heart. Maybe my entry was too different. It was a Ha-waiian quilt design. I don't know. Perhaps I should have sent a seascape, like my father suggested, or a copy of some famous artist's painting, as Mama wanted me to do." She sighed.

Bayard looked steadily down at the paint-ings. "Want my choice?" he asked.

"Of course. Please."

Quickly he pointed out two. One was a

scene at sunset, palm trees curved against a brilliant sky, a sailboat on the far horizon. The other was a small church surrounded by colorful red and pink anthuriums, the waxy, heart-shaped flower. "They show not only your skill but your emotion. The way you feel about the subject. Your heart. They *are* Hawaii."

Jana studied the paintings Bayard was pointing to. Immediately she knew he was right. She nodded. "Yes, I see what you mean."

"You really have talent, Jana. Scholarship or no scholarship, you should go on with it."

"Without one, I can't. Couldn't afford to go." Once the words were spoken, Jana could have bitten her tongue. She certainly didn't want to sound "poor mouth" to Bayard. However, he didn't seem to have even heard her. He had picked up one of the watercolors and was holding it at arm's length, examining it carefully.

"This is really good work, Jana. You can't give it up. Study abroad. You should go to France, to Paris."

"*Paris?* You are dreaming!" Jana gave him an incredulous look, thinking, *That's easy enough for* you *to say, Bayard.* People like the Prestons, people with money, never thought that the lack of it could make the difference between what you did and what you didn't do. Most of all, they didn't realize that money was necessary to fulfill dreams.

"But it would be a waste if you didn't continue." He caught her look, and a slow flush reddened under his tan. Still, he added seriously, "There must be a way."

"Oh sure, if you believe in Aladdin's lamp and have three wishes," she laughed, trying to lighten the moment.

"Could you leave this for a few minutes? Take a walk down to the beach with me? I have something to tell you."

His mood had changed abruptly. He had something on his mind. "Yes, of course. Just let me put these aside and stack the others. Mama is having her missionary society ladies' meeting here later."

Bayard was waiting for her outside when Jana came down the porch steps.

"Is something wrong?" she asked. "You look worried somehow."

"Not worried, exactly. Just sad. I have to go to the mainland. Father has arranged for me to take a position in a brokerage firm in New York. He wants me to learn investments so that I'll be able to take over when . . . he's gone."

"When are you going?" Jana asked, surprised that the thought of Bayard's leaving dismayed her. During the past few weeks, they had seen a great deal of each other. Her old impressions of him as being arrogant, conceited, self-centered, had gradually disappeared. She had come to know another Bayard, one she had never suspected. The bond between them *was* there, stronger than she had realized, and true — the deep love they shared of Hawaii.

"As soon as Father gets back and I can get my things together — a few weeks."

"Will you be here for my graduation?" she asked. Then, afraid that might have sounded too personal, she amended, "*Our* graduation, Akela's and mine."

"I wouldn't miss it," he assured her. They were at the gate and Bayard opened it. Together they walked a short distance to the small grove of banyan trees at the start of the path that led to the beach. Here Bayard halted.

"I hate to leave all this." His voice sounded strange, tight. "I think only *you* would understand that, Jana. I don't want to go. But I have to. I can't escape my responsibility."

"But you'll be coming back, Bayard. I mean, your father wants you to run the ranch, after all, doesn't he?"

Bayard nodded.

Her heart wrenched empathetically. She

did understand how he felt. She placed her hand on his arm and he turned toward her, then drew her into his arms, holding her tight against him. She felt his chin on her head as her cheek pressed against his chest. His hands smoothed her hair, and he murmured something she could not quite hear. Then he turned up her face and kissed her mouth. A slow, tender kiss. Sensing his need for comfort, Jana returned the kiss with a natural sweetness and sympathy. Bayard's arms tightened and he kissed her again. This time it was not gentle, but demanding — in it was a desperate longing that startled and then frightened her. Struggling out of his embrace, she stepped away from him, breathless. Her mouth felt bruised. Bayard dropped his arms and said, "I shouldn't have done that. I guess I want to hold on to something. You mean so much — symbolize all that I love. You're so special." He sighed heavily. "Now I have something else to apologize for, I suppose." The slightly sarcastic tone was back in his voice.

"No, not at all," she protested a little shakily. She wasn't blaming him, because she knew she had enjoyed his kiss. She had liked being held. For that moment, she had felt something wonderful. But was it for Bayard?

"I'd better go now," he said.

"Yes, and I have to get back home."

Silently they walked back up to the house. At the gate, Bayard took Jana's hand and held it in both of his for a moment. "Mahalo, Jana. For everything. For being you. I'll never forget the time we've spent together these last weeks."

Then he turned and walked away, and Jana went into the house. Inside she tiptoed down the hall, past the kitchen, where her mother was talking to Nathan, and to her room. She needed to be alone for a while to try to sort things out, analyze her feelings about what had just happened, about Bayard Preston.

She sat there on the edge of her bed, staring out at the darkening sky outside her window. The curve of the palm tree was silhouetted against a purple, mauve, and pink background.

The kiss had shaken her. Her response to it, even more so.

The time they had spent together these past few weeks had no reality, as if it were set apart from her normal life. It would be foolish to imagine a romantic relationship with someone like Bayard Preston. Who was under all that easy charm, the sophistication, the patina acquired by affluence and experience?

What would it be like to live within the magic circle of people like the Prestons? Bayard spoke so casually of going to Europe, and no expense had been too much for Colonel Preston to make sure Edith had her own horse at her prestigious school. Jana remembered the beautiful clothes Edith took so for granted, the lavishness of everything at the Preston Ranch. Her mind toyed with the idea of wealth, luxury, and travel.

Could she trust Bayard's enigmatic words? They were too vague, ambiguous. Had she been just a challenge, an interesting diversion? Yet there *was* something that drew them to each other, some strong attraction. But it wasn't love. Jana was sure it wasn't love. It couldn't be. Could it?

Fantastic daydreams invaded her thoughts. Dreams of being fashionably dressed, traveling to Europe, wandering through the vast halls of the great museums. . . . Bayard Preston could provide all this. If it was offered to her, would she turn it down?

Suddenly she thought of Kimo. It made her heart sore. Did he even remember what he'd written on the sand before he went away? In her heart of hearts she knew that no one else could fill the empty place he had left there.

"Jana!" her mother's voice called. "Come

set the table for supper."

Jana got up. What foolishness she had been thinking. She could not expect anyone to fulfill her dreams for her.

Graduation night was a beautiful mingling of traditional stateside and Hawaiian ceremony. The graduates were all in white — the girls in their prettiest dresses, the boys in embroidered shirts, white duck pants. All wore leis of red carnations and white plumeria, the school colors. There was an invocation by a well-known minister from Kona, a welcome from the principal to parents and friends of the graduates, the salutatory, the prize giving, the valedictorian's speech, and then the diplomas were handed out, the school song was sung, and everyone was invited for refreshments at the reception in the decorated gym.

The graduates formed a receiving line at the gym entrance. Jana had won the art prize and was happy to see Bayard in the crowd, coming up to congratulate her. She was pleased that he had come, pleased that he brought another lei to add to the several she was wearing. The gift of a lei on special occasions was a Hawaiian custom.

"May I walk you home?" he asked as he dropped the lovely garland of white and yellow hibiscus over her head.

It was a starry night and blissfully cool after the warmth of the crowded reception, where the air had been heavy with the scent of mixed flowers.

"I'm leaving day after tomorrow, Jana," Bayard told her.

"So soon?" Her disappointment sounded in her voice. "Just when I'll be free with no lessons, no deadlines to meet."

"Yes, I know. But . . ." Bayard shrugged. "But duty calls and all that nonsense." He sounded bitter. "I would have liked this time to go on, but Father has put everything into motion, and there's nothing I can do about it."

They walked back up to the house together in silence. At the gate Jana said, "The lei you brought is lovely, Bayard. Mahalo."

"I have something else for you, too," he said, putting his hand in his jacket pocket and bringing out a small, square package, wrapped and ribboned. He held it out to her. "I want you to have this."

She hesitated a moment, then took it. Her hands were already full with her diploma and her art prize.

"Don't open it now but after I'm gone. It's something I want you to have."

"Mahalo."

"Jana, I'm not sure when I'll be back. . . . I hate saying good-bye. I even hate saying good night." He laughed softly, then drew her into his arms, this time more gently than the other time. "I think I like the Hawaiian way best." He bent his head and kissed her the traditional way, once on each cheek. "Aloha." Then he was gone.

Jana stood there for a moment, looking into the darkness into which he had disappeared. In a few minutes she heard voices coming. Her parents were walking home with some friends and would soon be here. She wanted to be alone when she opened Bayard's gift, so she hurried into the house.

Once inside the house, she went straight to her room. She was trembling and didn't know exactly why. Excitement, probably. It had been a momentous evening. The end of a chapter in her life, the beginning of another.

It had been a wonderful evening. Only one important thing had been missing: Kimo. Her throat had ached when she saw all the Kipola family surrounding Akela, showering her with leis. Jana wished Kimo had been there. He would have brought her a lei, she was sure. But how could she be that certain? It had been so long, she could hardly remember what it was like when he had been here.

She understood now why she had responded to Bayard's kiss that evening. It was Kimo she had been longing to kiss when she was in Bayard's arms. She knew that was wrong. Unfair. But figuring that out had helped her put it into perspective.

That's why she wanted to open Bayard's present in private. She was afraid her mother would read too much into his gift. Perhaps, in a way, her mother might have liked to see her develop a romantic relationship with Bayard Preston. But Jana knew that would never happen. She was glad she had come to know Bayard in a different way, but it would never be that kind of love.

As soon as she unwrapped it and saw the name of the jeweler on the small silk box, she knew without opening it what it was. With shaky hands she lifted the lid, and there was the tiny shell pin with the one perfect pearl in its pale pink center. She drew in her breath. It looked even lovelier than it had when she first saw it in the display case.

Of course, she could not keep it. Not because her mother might think it improper for her to accept it, saying it was far too expensive a piece of jewelry for her to accept from a young man, *unless* . . .

But Jana herself knew why keeping it would be wrong. She and Bayard had used that very word "unless" and understood what it might mean. And there would be no *unless*. Not now, not ever. Not with Bayard Preston.

Jana snapped the little box closed. Keeping it was out of the question. And Bayard Preston was out of the question as well.

As Jana had expected, her mother said she must send it back. Jana rewrapped the present, wrote Bayard a note of thanks and regret, and mailed it to the Preston Ranch the next day. She did not hear from Bayard. Two days later she knew that he had left for Hilo.

Part 3

Chapter 18

When Jana heard that Edith Preston was coming home, she felt excited and yet a little anxious. She was afraid her own prediction that Edith would be drastically changed would prove true. Not only because of what Bayard had said about his sister but because of the fact that after her first few weeks at the Virginia school, neither Jana nor Akela had heard much from her. She seemed completely caught up in her new life on the mainland, her new friends, new activities. There had been a few notes, postcards, graduation gifts, but all the signs were that Edith's life had become a constant round of travel, theater, and weekend house parties.

The biggest shock and disappointment to Jana was that Edith had not seemed a bit homesick. In the two years she had been gone, she had not once come home to the Big Island. Instead, Colonel Preston had gone to the mainland twice, the last time for Bayard's graduation from Yale.

When Jana got the news, she confided some of her anxiety to Akela, hoping she might contradict her. "She'll probably be terribly changed," Jana said glumly. "She and her friends at that fancy school move in an entirely different world than we do. Edith could always afford to do things *we* could never do. But it's different now. She has friends with the same kind of money, who are able to do the same things she can. She spends time at *Newport, Rhode Island* — where only enormously wealthy people live, my mother says. They have *mansions* they call *summer cottages!* Edith will have nothing in common with *us* anymore."

Akela's smooth brow furrowed for a moment.

"Maybe not," she said complacently. "Maybe Kiki will be glad to be home. With *us*. Here where she can be herself. Not have to be something everyone expects. I imagine she has to 'pretend' a great deal with her friends over there. Especially because they don't know or understand anything about Hawaii."

"Maybe you're right, but I'm not so sure," Jana said doubtfully.

All her fears came to a climax a week later.

Edith came tearing into the Rutherfords' yard on her horse, jumped down from her saddle, and ran up the steps onto the porch, calling, "Jana! Jana! Where are you? I'm home!"

Jana was sitting at her bedroom window, sketching. At the sound of that familiar voice, she jumped up, spilling her sketchbook to the floor, upsetting her brushes, overturning her water jar. Replacing everything in quick movements, Jana dashed out the door. She heard her mother's voice greet Edith, and Edith's enthusiastic response. In the hallway, Jana halted, feeling all at once strangely shy. Then Edith, standing just inside the front door, turned and saw her. "Jana!" she shrieked and rushed toward her.

The two girls hugged, then grabbed each other around the waist and danced together down the length of the hallway.

"Oh, Kiki! I'm so glad to see you!"

"Oh, I'm so glad to be back. You can't imagine!" screamed Edith, laughing merrily. "I'd forgotten what heaven Hawaii is! I leaned over the ship's railing so far, Papa kept worrying I'd fall over as we came into the harbor."

Jana took a step back, still holding Edith's shoulders, regarding her speculatively.

Dressed in a blue cotton shirt, a divided riding skirt, she looked just the same. The carelessly tied ribbon on her straw hat had loosened and had fallen back, letting her fair hair tumble about her shoulders. All Jana's apprehensions about a changed friendship faded. The old Kiki she remembered was back, just the same lovable, harum-scarum girl as ever.

They tethered Edith's mare in the shade of a sprawling banyan tree beside the Rutherfords' house, then trudged down the road and up the hill to Tutu Kipola's house to see Akela. On the way, Edith asked anxiously, "How is she? All the time I was away at school, I worried that you two would forget all about me. That when I came home, you would have changed, wouldn't want me as a friend anymore."

"How funny!" Jana stopped short and looked at Edith in amazement. "That's exactly what *we* thought might happen with *you!*"

"Really? Well, you two were always so close. I mean, before I came to school, you and Akela were best friends. I wasn't sure if you'd accept me, and then you did —" She shrugged. "But when I went away, I just thought — well, maybe I was afraid that after I was gone so long . . ."

Jana slipped her hand through Edith's arm. "No way! Never. Remember what we always said: 'A threefold cord is not easily broken'? We'll always be friends, no matter what."

"And how about Kimo?" was Edith's next question.

Jana's face got warm in spite of her not wanting to reveal too much to her sharp-eyed companion.

"Kimo is in Germany, didn't you know? He got a two-year apprenticeship with a famous cabinetmaker. He won't be home again for I'm not sure how long."

"I didn't know. I just remember him showing up at the rodeo at our house party that Christmas." She looked sideways at Jana. "You saw him that summer, didn't you?"

"No, he left for Germany right from Honolulu. It's a very long trip, you know." Jana tried to sound casual. "Kimo was always good-looking."

"You should hear what the girls at my school say about him when I've shown them pictures!" Edith laughed gaily. "They roll their eyes, pretend to faint, and giggle like crazy! They call him the 'noble savage,' from that picture of him dressed up as King Kahmehameha in our eighth-grade May Day pageant."

"How stupid!" Jana reacted indignantly. "I never knew anyone less like a savage than Kimo. He's the most gentle, kindest, most soft-spoken person in the world."

Edith looked at her with a startled expression. "Why are you getting your dander up? It was meant as a compliment —"

"Well, it certainly didn't sound like one," Jana retorted huffily. "What do those girls know about Hawaiians, anyway? To make such a remark."

"Jana! It's nothing to get upset about."

"It does upset me." Jana tossed her head. "Kimo is so intelligent and talented and well read. To make snap judgments about someone you don't even know seems — well, pretty *ignorant* of them."

"I'm sorry I said anything. I certainly didn't mean to offend you."

"It's not *me*, it's Kimo."

"But *you're* the one taking offense."

"Well, he's not here to defend himself. I should think *you* would have defended him when those silly girls made that comment."

Edith stopped walking, turned and faced Jana.

"Listen, Jana, I'm sorry. For whatever I said or did — or didn't say or do! Don't let's quarrel, for heaven's sake. It's my first day home. Please."

Jana felt ashamed and somewhat embarrassed by her outburst. "I'm sorry, too," she mumbled.

"Is there something you're not telling me?" Edith asked quietly. "Something about Kimo — and you? You love him, don't you?"

Jana met her friend's eyes slowly. "Of course I love him."

"And not like a brother, right?"

"Oh, I don't know, Kiki. He's been gone a long time. I don't know how he feels or — I suppose you'd say, as a dear friend."

"*More* than a friend?" Edith persisted.

Whatever more she was going to ask was interrupted by a voice calling to them from the top of the hill. Jana turned and, seeing a figure in a wide-brimmed straw hat and colorful mumu standing there, said, "There's Tutu. Let's hurry."

That afternoon, it *did* seem like old times. The three girls had a happy reunion. Edith left earlier than Jana, saying that she had to stop at the post office for the ranch mail and that her father expected her home for dinner.

After she was gone, Akela gently chided Jana. "See, what did I tell you? Wasn't Kiki just the same as she used to be? I didn't think she'd changed a bit."

Jana did not comment. She herself had sensed something different about Edith. She didn't talk much about her life at school, on the mainland, or with her new friends. Instead, she seemed happy just to do the things the three of them had always done.

Jana soon dismissed the idea that her friend had changed. But even during the occasional times they spent alone together without Akela, Jana felt there was something held back, something Edith wasn't quite ready to open up about, even to her close friend.

That is, until one afternoon when Edith arrived at the Rutherfords' house quivering with suppressed excitement. Her dark eyes were shining. "I have something wonderful to tell you, Jana. You first, because you were in on it from the beginning. But it hasn't been easy to bring off. I had to come clear home — but it worked! Look, *look!*" She thrust out her left hand and wiggled the third finger, on which a large emerald ring sparkled. "I'm engaged!"

"What?" gasped Jana.

"I couldn't wait to tell you. I can hardly believe it myself."

Jana glanced from the ring to Edith's radiant face.

"Yes, yes, it's true. I'm going to be married. To Greg Amory."

"Greg Amory," Jana repeated. Of Bayard's chums at the house party, Greg was the one she had liked least. She almost exclaimed, "Oh no, not *him!*" Then she remembered that Edith had set out to capture his heart, had mapped out a whole campaign. She must have continued to pursue him when she was on the mainland.

"Remember how *smitten* I was with him at the time? He was so . . . so sophisticated, so aloof. I didn't want to make a fool of myself. But I played my cards just right. I told him that if he wasn't serious, I was going home to the island and not ever coming back to the States. I wasn't even sure when I left if it would work. But it did. I got letters, and then — it happened." Edith snapped her fingers. "He sent the ring. It came by insured mail this morning!" She laughed delightedly. "It's taken me a long time to catch him. But *persistence* won the day! Oh Jana, I'm so excited, so thrilled. He is so handsome — you do remember, don't you? Tall, blonde. He's captain of the tennis team at college and — oh well, so many things. And he thinks that" — she threw back her head, laughing — "I'm adorable. Can you imagine?"

"But isn't this all — well, awfully sudden?"

"Well, no, not really." She pulled a face. "I thought I'd better act quick. Before he changed his mind!" She laughed again, a laugh that sounded a little high and forced to Jana. "You see, he was planning to go to England for a year, travel on the continent. I was afraid he might meet someone going over — you've heard of those shipboard romances! Anyway, Greg's parents were sending him abroad and — well, you just never know. Well, Bayard and I were invited to their home on Long Island Sound. It was then that I worked all my magic." Edith looked down at her ring again, holding it out so it glittered. She admired it for a minute before she rushed on, saying, "But I also issued my ultimatum. . . ."

Jana found herself speechless, unable to think of anything appropriate to say. Somehow Greg Amory, at least the Greg she remembered, was not — *could* not be — right for Edith. Could he? Before she could think this through further, Edith said something that halted her cold.

"It was a romantic weekend all around." She glanced at Jana, her dimples showing. "No one was immune, including Bayard. Actually, Bayard has been seeing quite a lot of my roommate, Vinnie Albright, who is a friend of Greg's sister, Katherine. As a matter of fact, both she and Katherine will be my bridesmaids. And of course you and Akela will, too."

At this Jana felt her heart pinch. Bayard?

It was too much for Jana to take in all at once. She tried to listen as Edith went into the plans for the wedding, explaining that her Aunt Ruthie was coming from San Francisco to oversee the details. However, Jana's mind was like a phonograph record with the needle stuck in place. Edith's casual reference to Bayard being romantically interested in Vinnie Albright kept playing itself over and over. After all the things he had said to her — about Edith's mainland friends, about how different and refreshing he found *her*. Yes, Bayard had said a great many things. Maybe none of them should have been believed. But in spite of herself, Jana felt hurt.

If she had been taken in by Bayard's flattering attention those few weeks he was here in the spring, it was her own fault. The whole rather intense time might have been a combination of his own unsettledness and the fact that she had been there.

Edith's voice brought her back to the present. "We've set a date six weeks from now. Not much time to plan everything. But Aunt Ruthie will be here soon to help arrange it all. I've already decided that I'll wear my mother's wedding gown. It will have to be altered a little to fit me. Just wait until you see it, Jana. It's simply gorgeous — yards of Brussels lace over ivory satin, the train six feet long and embroidered with seed pearls. I've also decided on the bridesmaids' gowns — different pastel shades to suit each one's coloring. Yours and Akela's will be perfect for you both. Yours will be a lovely color of blue to match your eyes, and Akela's will be a deep rose. . . ." Edith rambled on and on about the wedding while Jana only half listened. It still seemed incredible. A restlessness about this marriage stirred in her spirit. It was an uneasiness she couldn't explain, yet she felt it deeply. But Edith was so deliriously happy. . . .

"Come, let's go over to Akela's. I want to tell her too and show her my ring," giggled Edith, flinging out her arm dramatically and wiggling her finger so that the stone's facets danced in the sun.

Later, after their visit with Akela, Edith and Jana walked back down the hill to the Rutherfords' house. On the way, Edith squeezed Jana's arm and said, "Isn't it thrilling, like something out of a dream or a romance novel? But all this is really happening to me. It's like a kind of fairy story, with a prince falling in love with me."

But Edith Preston was certainly not a Cinderella, even though she might have been treated like a princess all her life. Neither did Jana think Greg Amory was any Prince Charming. In fact, Jana thought he was a spoiled, self-indulgent rich boy. Could these two possibly find happiness together? For Edith's sake, she hoped so.

"We are going to Europe, Jana, on our honeymoon," Edith rattled on. "Just think, I'll see Paris, Florence, Rome! I'll visit all the galleries and museums for you!" She jumped up. "I must be going. Aunt Ruthie is coming, did I tell you? She'll be here until the wedding to see to all the details. Papa says I'm not competent now that I'm out of my head in love," she laughed gaily. "Greg won't come until the week of the wedding. Come up to the ranch tomorrow and you can sketch my idea for the bridesmaids' dresses so we can give them to Aunt Ruthie. She'll have her wonderful seamstress, who does the most exquisite work, make them."

How long had Edith secretly been planning this? Jana wondered. Greg Amory never had a chance. Once Edith set her mind on something, she either got her way or else.

"See you tomorrow!" Edith gave Jana an impulsive hug, and then she was gone.

Jana went inside the house, then decided to walk down to the beach. That was where she did most of her "heavy thinking." And today she had plenty to do.

She sat on the sand, her arms locked around her knees, looking out at the ever-rolling surf. As it usually did at the beach, time passed almost unnoticed. Her mind turned over all the changes that had happened in just the past two years. Kimo in Germany, Akela and Pelo in love, and now Edith planning to marry. And she would be going away herself, to the mainland. Either to teachers college or art school — she had not heard definitely yet.

Childhood was gone and with it her childhood friends, each taking his or her own path, leading to individual destinies. What would become of them all?

Jana thought about Bayard, what Edith had told her about him and Vinnie Albright. She remembered his kisses and what he had said that last night — "I'll never forget our time together" — and she thought about the gift he had wanted to give her, the lovely shell pin with the pearl.

After he was gone, Jana had rarely heard from him. There were no impassioned love letters to keep alive the flame that had briefly flared between them. Perhaps it had burned brightly for a moment in time and quickly flickered out.

Jana examined her own reasons for being caught up in that fleeting romantic interlude. Deep down she had never really believed anything would come of it. Perhaps Bayard could not help himself. Through Edith, Jana had always heard of Bayard's many romantic escapades. Every vacation that he was home, on his bureau were letters, a new framed picture of still another young lady he was courting.

She could explain her own attraction to Bayard. His easy charm was very appealing, and he had a way with words, an ability to make you feel you were the only person in the room — for a while. What girl would not be flattered?

However, in her heart of hearts Jana understood that someone like Bayard could never give her what she longed for — an enduring love, devotion, faithfulness. He wasn't capable of that kind of love. Maybe he realized that to Jana he would have to offer something more than he could give.

Jana truly believed that for some people,

there is only one deep, passionate love in a lifetime. Whether that love is fulfilled or unrequited, the memory of such a love will give sweetness and strength to all one's days. That's the only kind she wanted, the kind she would wait to have.

Slowly the sun lowered, turning the sea to a gray-blue polished glass. It was time for her to leave, go back up to the house. She only wished she could feel happier about Edith.

The day of Edith's wedding was perfect in only the way one can be in Hawaii. A soft ocean breeze wafted up gently, stirring the flower-scented air. The ranch could have been a stage setting. On the lawn, an expanse of green grass was like a velvety carpet rolled out from the house. White folding chairs had been set in semicircular rows before a flower-decked trellis, where the wedding was to take place. All through the trees that lined the driveway, decorated paper lanterns were hung to be lit after sunset. By noon the musicians began arriving, settling themselves on the platform stand, tuning their instruments in preparation for playing traditional wedding music during the ceremony and providing a background of island music for the reception that would follow. Colonel Preston had hired a well-known vocalist to sing some of the most popular songs, to the accompaniment of the soft strumming of guitar and ukulele.

In the house, servants moved quickly and quietly on the main floor, moving in trained competence as they arranged long refreshment tables, placed the floral centerpieces, polished the crystal glasses. Even though this was their young mistress' wedding party, their efficiency was unaffected by the special importance of the occasion, as Preston Ranch had held many grand fetes, had entertained royalty, both Hawaiian and European.

Upstairs, in contrast, was all hustle and bustle. Edith had invited Akela and Jana to come to the ranch to dress. The other bridesmaids — Katherine Amory, Greg's sister; Maevis Latham, one of Edith's suitemates at the Virginia school she attended; and Vinnie Albright, Edith's roommate — were staying in one of the guest cottages and would dress there.

Jana was glad of that. She'd had about all she could stand of the fluttery threesome from the mainland. Katherine Amory was very much like her brother — a cool blond with an aloof manner. Maevis was sweet but rather dull, the perfect foil for Edith's vivacious personality. What other type could have put up with such competition? Vinnie Albright was another matter. Jana was surprised at the sharp twinge of jealousy she felt when she was introduced. She grudgingly had to admit that the vivid brunette was extremely pretty. She had a witty tongue and a poise that could only come from a certain eastern shore background. Jana could see why she would be attractive to someone like Bayard.

At the prenuptial festivities, Jana had tried to avoid both of them. That hadn't proved difficult. Bayard had also seemed to be avoiding her.

Was he embarrassed or uncomfortable? That was his problem, she told herself. In a way, it made her feel superior. She was proud that she could handle an awkward situation with more grace than he could.

Bayard and Greg were occupying one of the guest cottages, and so when Jana had arrived at the ranch, she had gone through the house and upstairs without encountering either. As she reached the top of the steps, she could hear her friend's laughter ringing out, and Akela's softer voice. Unbidden, a lump rose in her throat. This would be the last time the three of them would be together in the same way. After today nothing would ever be the same. Determined not to let any feelings of sadness overshadow what should be a shining moment for Edith, Jana winked back tears. Just then Edith had come running barefoot down the hall.

She had greeted Jana enthusiastically with a hug and pulled her along by the hand to her bedroom. "You must see my gown!"

Gazing at the beautiful dress hanging from the armoire, Jana had given Edith the reaction she wanted. "I've never seen anything more beautiful!"

Edith's usual high spirits today were at their peak — sometimes her tendency to dissolve into giggles bordered dangerously on the brink of hysteria. Meipala's expression was concerned, her dark eyes worried, as she hovered anxiously. Jana, always sensitive to undercurrents, was aware that her friend was teetering on doing something reckless. She had the wild thought that maybe Edith would dash out of the room, out to the stables, get on her horse, and ride off. She quickly thrust that possibility away. She gave Akela a warning glance, and they both tried to exert a little calm.

"It's only natural to feel nervous," Akela began as they all sat on Edith's bed, enjoying the jasmine tea and thin ginger cookies Meipala had left on a tray before going downstairs.

"Why should I be nervous?" demanded Edith, tossing her head. "I absolutely adore Greg, and he adores me! We are going to be divinely happy!"

And why shouldn't they be? Jana asked herself. No two people were starting out together with more potential for happiness — they had youth, wealth, health. Why this nagging feeling that Edith's expectations were too high for her not to be disillusioned or disappointed?

Jana hoped this wouldn't happen, prayed it wouldn't. Edith had been so caught up in the elaborate preparations for the extravagant wedding — picking out the "exactly right" engraved invitations, selecting her china, her silver, the fittings for her trousseau — she'd had no time to consider what followed: the reality of living with another person for the rest of her life, day after day, year after year. Was the man she was marrying right for her? Jana still had her doubts. Jana could also not help wondering what was going through Greg Amory's mind at this point.

Meipala's head peered into the bedroom. "Time to get ready, girls."

They made a scramble to uncurl themselves from their perches on the bed. Akela and Jana left Edith to the ministrations of her old nurse and went into the adjoining bedroom.

"I hope — I hope she's doing the right thing," Jana whispered.

At the tone of doubt in Jana's voice, Akela's dark eyes widened. "She seems to be very much in love."

"I know, but —" Jana hesitated. "I wish I felt more sure."

"Tutu says that only the two people involved know. Everyone else looks on the outside — *they* know their hearts."

"It's easier for you, Akela. You and Pelo. You've grown up together, practically in the same family — you have the same kind of childhood, the same traditions, and you want the same kind of life." Jana shook her head slowly. "Greg Amory comes from an entirely different world. I just want Edith to be happy."

Akela reached out and pressed Jana's hand. "She will be, don't worry. Love between two people is very powerful. It can change things, make differences seem unimportant."

Jana wished she could share Akela's confidence.

There was no time to discuss it further. The wedding was scheduled for five o'clock. That time was especially picked because the garden would be golden with the glow of an early sunset, enhancing everything with glorious light.

Akela helped Jana with her hair, and then Jana did hers. Their dresses had been chosen in the most becoming color for each. Their picture hats were flattering, the curved brims lined with shirred pink chiffon. At last came a knock at the door and Meipala's voice reminding them it was time to go downstairs.

The other three bridesmaids were gathered in the library, whose French doors opened onto the lanai. As Akela and Jana joined them, there were exchanged murmurs of mutual admiration. Then a kind of expectant hush fell over them as they waited for Edith. When she appeared on Colonel Preston's arm, they all drew a collective awed breath. The Edith they knew had been transformed into a vision of a bride. Under the voluminous tulle veil that covered her face, they could see she was smiling. Her gown was a dream of shimmering satin, embroidered and outlined in tiny pearls. Before they had a chance to say anything, Colonel Preston declared proudly, "Was there ever such a beautiful bride?"

There were a few moments of emotional flurry, and then Meipala handed them their bouquets. From outside they could hear the strains of lovely Hawaiian music. Through the open doors, they saw that most of the seats were full. Between the rows was a path for the bridal party, which led to the flower-banked podium, where the surpliced and black-cassocked priest, prayer book in hand, waited. At his side stood Greg and Bayard, looking erect and handsome in white linen suits. Even though she had schooled herself against Bayard's charms and found it difficult to excuse Greg's superficiality, Jana had to admit that the two tall, blond young men could have modeled for a picture of a pair of Grecian gods from some Athenian temple.

The ceremony, the reception, even the fact that she had caught the bridal bouquet, did not lift Jana's spirits to the level such an event should have. She tried her best to enter into the festivities, to laugh, to chat, to join in the toasts to bride and groom, to dance with Greg's cousin, who seemed very attracted, and at the end of the evening to pelt the couple with flower petals as they ran hand in hand to the new carriage that would take them away on their honeymoon.

Later, when she was finally home, in her own room, easing her tired feet out of her blue satin slippers, Jana felt as lonely as she had ever been. She glanced at the beautiful bridal bouquet that, she was convinced, Edith had aimed directly at her, and sighed. Her emotions were a mixture of pleasure and pain. Jana had not mistaken the meaning of the distance Bayard had kept from her. It had really needed no explanation, because when she had entered the library where the bridesmaids were assembled, she could not miss seeing the small shell pin with the tiny pearl Vinnie Albright was wearing on the bodice of her bridesmaid's dress.

Today had been the end of one part of her life. She did not know what the next chapter would bring. All she could hope was that Kimo would be in it.

Two weeks after Edith's wedding, in the island newspaper appeared the announcement of Bayard Preston's engagement to Vinnie Albright.

Part 4

Capter 19

With Edith married and gone, Kimo far away in Germany, and Akela spending most of her time in Kona, preoccupied with Pelo and planning a December wedding, Jana found herself lonelier than she had ever been before in her life.

Because of the Rutherfords' financial situation, it was decided Jana would have to wait another year to go to teachers college on the mainland. Even if she was aided by a partial scholarship, there were other expenses to be met. Although her parents came to this decision regretfully, Jana actually did not mind. She still hoped that she might win a scholarship to art school.

Besides, she had been asked to be a bridesmaid in Akela and Pelo's wedding, the only one outside their immediate family to be included in the bridal party. The Hawaiian *ohana* was very intimate and close. Most of the other bridal attendants were

Akela's cousins, so Jana felt honored to have been chosen.

Jana wondered if Kimo would return in time for the wedding. No one, not even Tutu, knew for sure when he would get home from Germany. Jana had kept all the postcards he had sent her, but two years was a long while. Sometimes their moments together seemed unreal — sometimes she could hardly remember what he looked like or what they had talked about. More and more, the romantic dreams she had after his last visit home gradually faded. Perhaps he had met someone in Germany he cared about. Perhaps . . .

In the meantime, she took a job clerking at the fabric store in Waimea, putting aside most of her small salary to save for college.

She kept busy with her job and helped her mother around the house, trying to make herself useful, and in her free time she painted. She took on Nathan's Sunday school class, since there was no one else in the small congregation who volunteered, and to her surprise found she liked it.

Not often, but once in a while, her thoughts strayed to Bayard Preston and the brief interlude they had shared. Had he really considered pursuing a romantic relationship with her? Or had he already decided that a prestigious marriage with a socialite like Vinnie Albright was more advantageous? She was happy she had not been dazzled too much by his charm and all he might have offered. In her heart of hearts she knew they were "unequally yoked."

She also tried not to put too much importance on her memories of Kimo. Perhaps she kept thinking of him because right now her life seemed empty. She tried not to envy Akela's happiness or Edith's glamorous life.

Maybe her life was going to be different from her friends' lives. Maybe she would never marry, just live in a cottage on a hillside overlooking the ocean, with a small studio where she could paint. While Edith toured Europe in style and Akela became a traditional Hawaiian wife whose duties were her husband's comfort and contentment, *she* would live alone and become a famous artist — a reclusive one!

The morning of Akela's wedding, Jana arrived at Tutu's house. She found a radiant Akela. Never before had she seemed so beautiful. Her inner beauty shone from her luminous dark eyes. The two friends embraced and Jana had to fight the lump rising in her throat. She remembered the first time she had ever seen Akela. She had looked like a small, exotic doll. Akela and Kimo had been fellow boarders at the Caldwells' house while Jana's parents were in Honolulu and Tutu was in Kohala at the bedside of a sick family member. Jana recalled how quickly she and Akela had become friends, and all the walks, the talks, the confidences shared, the secrets kept over the years. They had been like sisters. Now she was losing her. It would never be the same again.

Not wanting to spoil her friend's day, Jana held back tears, entering into all the last-minute activities with affection and enthusiasm.

Since Akela and Pelo were both Christians, there would first be a wedding ceremony in Tutu's church, where Akela had worshiped as a child and still did, except for the weekends she spent in Kona. This would be followed by a traditional Hawaiian exchange of vows, and a *luau* on the beach. That way, any of the bride and groom's friends who could not be squeezed into the tiny church would not feel left out.

Akela's bridal gown was an exquisitely embroidered white muslin dress fashioned with a high neck. The long, tapered sleeves were puffed at the top and had wrists that were edged in delicate lace. A train fell from the shoulders in panels of ruffles. She wore a wreath of fresh flowers. Her long, dark hair hung loose, and around her neck was the traditional ti-leaf lei.

When it was time for them to go to the church, a wagon decorated by the family with garlands of flowers and driven by one of the male cousins drew up in front of Tutu's cottage. Tutu helped settle Akela carefully in front, arranging her train, and then Jana and the four other bridesmaids, Akela's pretty, giggling cousins, climbed in, and they started off down the hill to the church.

As they stopped in the churchyard, a crowd was already waiting for the bride's arrival. Through the open church door, they heard the wheezing sound of the old organ playing some of the beloved old hymns. Now quiet, subdued with the solemnity of the occasion, they all got out of the wagon and went up the steps. At the top, waiting on the porch, was Uncle Kelo, who was to give Akela away. He greeted them all with an "Aloha" and a hug and kiss, then held out his arm to Akela. She took it but not before she turned and stretched out her hand to grasp Jana's, squeezing it hard. Then the squeaky notes of "The Wedding March" sounded. The bridesmaids followed Tutu, then slowly marched down the aisle in the church, which was bedecked with flowers and crowded to the walls with smiling people.

During the ceremony, Jana had an entirely different reaction than she'd had at Edith's wedding only months before. She'd had so many doubts about Edith's happiness with Greg Amory — she had none at all for Akela.

Hearing the words of the vows her friend was taking, Jana knew they were promises she herself longed to make. But only with a man she could love and trust. Would it ever happen for her?

The ceremony over, the bridal party went out into the bright sunshine to gather on the church steps for the photography session. The jovial photographer kept rearranging them until all were laughing. Their laughter was a mixture of irritation and resignation, because they were all eager to get to the gala luau still ahead. Finally satisfied, he released them, and they all scattered among the assembled well-wishers in the churchyard. The bride and groom were swallowed up in the crowd, which showered them with congratulations and loaded them with leis.

Eventually, as if by some silent signal, everyone started on foot down the path to the beach below, where they could already smell the tantalizing aroma of the roasting meat being prepared for the upcoming feast.

Pelo's brothers and cousins had been up before dawn getting the pork ready to be roasted in the specially dug pit. A delicious herb-seasoned aroma rose with the spiraling smoke, prickling nostrils and whetting appetites. Tables were arranged in a large U-shape, decorated with piles of fruit and flowers, loaded with dishes of sweet potatoes, rice, and salads, and hovered over by colorfully mumu-clad "aunties" in flower-bedecked straw hats. Mats were placed on the sand, and groups of guests, friends, and families were settling themselves for the entertainment that would come later.

The scene might have been some exotic painting, Jana thought. She looked around at the gaily dressed company. Under the shade of the curved palm trees, their jagged-edged fronds languidly moving in the gentle sea wind, were clusters of guests happily chatting. Beyond the white-sand beach, the water of the lagoon stretched in rippling shades of blue, turquoise, jade. Down at the edge of the ocean, scores of little brown-skinned children played, shrieking as they chased each other, waded, and fell full length in the shallow waves. Their mothers and tutus sat not far away, watching them with tender tolerance.

Hawaiians were so joyous, so light-hearted, enjoying everything with a kind of happy nonchalance that Jana found most appealing. There was no stiffness, no studied awareness of social protocol to be observed — just simply living in the moment.

At last the meat was ready, and everyone began to serve themselves from the abundance set out: the tender white fish, freshly caught; the piping hot *laulaus,* seasoned meat wrapped in leaves and baked; and of course, inevitably, a huge bowl of poi set in the middle of the table for everyone to dip from. As Jana skipped putting any on her plate, she caught the eye of Uncle Kelo, Tutu's brother, who winked at her broadly. Although through the years, especially when Kimo was present, Jana had managed to take some of the gluey taro and swallow it, it was not her favorite Hawaiian delicacy.

While everyone ate and talked, the drums began to play softly. There were drums of all shapes and sizes, gourds, coconut shells. Gradually the beat began getting steadily louder, until it filled the air with an insistent rhythm impossible to ignore. A murmur went through the crowd. Soon the dancers would begin. Young men and women seemed to emerge as if by magic from the grove of banyans to a place in front of where the diners were seated. The girls were dressed in *sarongs*, lengths of flowered material in bold designs of red, yellow, and black, one end brought up over the shoulder, caught up and knotted at the hips. The dance was the traditional Hawaiian *hula-hula*, the slow, graceful telling of legends, the hand motions spelling out the story to those who understood the signs.

It was mesmerizing to watch, the music haunting. The spectators could not keep themselves from swaying or beating their hands on their knees to the rhythm of the drums.

Behind the dancers, the sun began dropping — a huge, orange ball — into the now glazed, silver-toned sea.

Jana hated to see this beautiful day come to an end. She wished it would go on and on, but the wind off the ocean became cooler, the shadows of the palm trees fell gently on the sand. It was time to go. Unnoticed, the wedding couple had slipped away, and the other guests were gathering up their children, baskets, belongings, preparing to leave the beach.

As the last plaintive notes of the guitars, ukuleles, and drums echoed in the balmy air, Jana felt a strange ache, her heart hungry, her soul a little lonely. Something within her yearned to belong to this culture, so simple, so sweet. As she reluctantly said her good-byes to Akela's family and turned to retrace her steps up the path to the church, a voice behind her spoke.

"Aloha, Koana."

Unbelievingly, she whirled around and saw Kimo.

At first she was speechless. Then words tumbled out, one on top of the other.

"Kimo! What are you doing here? When did you come?"

"Just now. I tried to make it for the wedding, but the steamer from Oahu was late. Then I had to get a ride from the dock, and — well, it looks like I've missed everything." He paused, then smiled broadly. "Except you."

"Why didn't you let anyone know? We could have met you —"

"I wanted to surprise everyone. Especially Akela and Pelo —" He stopped, looked around. "It seems everyone has gone."

Jana followed his glance. A few groups were left. Parents were collecting their children, some of whom were playing hide-and-seek and pretending not to hear their mothers calling them.

"I've seen Tutu. She's going home with Uncle Kelo. So may I walk you home?" he asked her.

Suddenly Jana's earlier melancholy vanished. Kimo was back and their meeting was just as she had imagined it, only better.

Chapter 20

With the evening of Akela's wedding and Kimo's return, Jana's life took a decided upward turn. Kimo's first few weeks after coming back from Germany were spent visiting his large family of relatives. However, he found plenty of time to see Jana. He would come to the store at closing time, and they would walk home the long way, going down the beach. The awkwardness she had feared after their long time apart never materialized. They found they had much to say to each other. It seemed as if all the years of separation had been like waters dammed up for a long time but now let flow. Kimo told her of what it was like to be a hardworking apprentice in a foreign land, learning a new language, a new way of communicating with people, while learning all kinds of new skills.

"It was different than when I was at school in Honolulu," he told her. "There I was among my own race, other Hawaiians. Even though we all came from different towns, even from different islands — some were from Kauai and Maui — still we were all Hawaiians. In Germany it was different. Sometimes I felt very alone."

"I wish I'd known —"

"I didn't want to write, worry Tutu or anybody. It seemed better just to work hard. That way, the time would pass faster. Push the loneliness back. Suppress it, get on with what I had to do."

"I'm so sorry, Kimo. If I'd known, maybe I could have helped somehow. Written to you about things here —"

He shook his head. "No, that would have hurt too much. It was probably better this way. I managed. Most people were kind, and my master's family tried to help. Actually, they were very kind to us — the apprentices. Had us to their house for dinner." Kimo made a face. "The food, though. Very heavy, very rich."

"It must have been really hard."

"It was. At least at first. But I learned a great deal. Not only in woodworking. I had to learn the language, of course, to understand directions, just to get along every day. And German is a hard language to learn." He laughed. "Maybe especially for a Hawaiian. It is very precise, very practical. Just like the Germans."

Jana recalled how she had once said that Kimo's woodwork was like poetry.

"No poetry, then?" she suggested softly.

He looked surprised that she had remembered that. "Of a sort. German woodworkers have their own poetry. Of course, it's different than mine. Poetry comes from the soul, and each country has a different kind of soul. Different doesn't mean inferior — just different. However, it was a valuable experience. I got a lot out of it. Things I intend to apply to my own work here."

"Then, you're going to stay here? Not go away again?"

Again Kimo seemed surprised at her question. "Of course. Hawaii's my home. Why would I want to go anywhere else?"

Jana's heart leaped. That was just how *she* felt.

"I don't plan to *ever* go away again," Kimo said definitely. "I will do my own designs, make them out of native wood, become a master woodworker here on the island."

"Oh, that's wonderful, Kimo. I'm so glad." Jana sighed. "I was afraid. People assumed you might either stay on in Germany or go to the mainland."

"I don't know why they'd think that. I'd never do such a thing. I was so glad to get home. To see Tutu, my family —" He paused. "And *you*, Koana. I thought about you all the time. I missed you more than you know."

As it turned out, within weeks Kimo and two other woodworkers formed a cooperative, opening a carpentry business together in Hilo. It would be slow going at first, but all three men did outstanding work. They were all ambitious and hardworking, and they hoped that soon more orders would begin to come in as their work became known.

It was only on weekends that Kimo and Jana could spend uninterrupted time together. They usually met after church and took long walks on the beach. They found they could talk to each other about almost everything. Sometimes their conversation turned serious.

Jana discovered that Kimo had become politicized. He and his coworkers often discussed the future of the Hawaiian islands. They were afraid, he told her, that little by little Hawaii was being taken over by foreigners, was losing its sovereignty. They felt that Hawaii should be for Hawaiians, not for the English or the Americans.

"I don't understand. Isn't it?"

"The Americans have too much influence, want power. Besides, Americans do not accept Hawaiians as equals."

"What do you mean? My parents are Americans, and so are the Prestons. They don't feel that way, I'm sure."

"Maybe not on the Big Island. But elsewhere. I've traveled in the States, on the mainland, Jana. I've seen things firsthand. Americans have prejudice against dark-skinned people. I experienced some of it myself. Nothing bad. Just a few curious looks. Still, I felt it."

Jana felt an inner rage. She knew enough history to be aware of the treatment of blacks that had led to the Civil War in the United States. But that was over now. It couldn't be that someone like Kimo, the descendant of kings, although dark haired and bronzed of skin, could be considered inferior by Americans or by *anybody!*

"I wish the queen had more Hawaiians as advisors," Kimo continued. "Right now she is surrounded by men who have their own influence to peddle. She has some powerful enemies."

"But if royalty cannot rule well, wouldn't it be better to have good counsel?"

"As long as their motives are pure." Kimo shook his head. "I don't have the answers — I just know we should have our own people deciding things for us. I don't like to see my country exploited."

Not all their conversations were of this depth. Something else was happening between them. It was on these walks, in this time they spent together, that their childhood friendship and youthful uncertainty with each other began to develop into something deeper. Perhaps Jana knew it first. She realized that the girlish attraction she'd had for Kimo was now much more. The handsome boy she had admired had become a man of strength, character, and integrity. The kind of man she could love with the kind of love that would endure for a lifetime.

With Kimo back, everything was just as she often had imagined it would be, had hoped it would be, only it was better. They seemed to have reached a new level of relationship. Jana did not yet dare call it love, because she was unsure of Kimo's feelings.

The cooperative Kimo kept very busy. The three men had to work very hard to earn enough to cover the rental of their shop, pay supply bills, and meet other expenses. Orders were slow coming in at first, and they sometimes had to take other work, plain carpentry, to make ends meet. It seemed a shame to Jana for Kimo to work on ordinary things, when his own designs were truly "poetry in wood." However,

Kimo remained optimistic about his future. His dream was to one day have his own shop in Waimea or Kona where he could create beautiful original furniture.

Sometimes he wasn't able to get home for the weekend. Other times he surprised Jana by showing up unexpectedly. A kind of telepathy developed between them. If he arrived too late to attend the Sunday service, she would often get a feeling of his presence, and when she came outside, she would find him waiting in the churchyard. The growing bond between them was difficult to explain but very real, and it grew stronger and stronger.

Jana was unaware that anyone else noticed how often they were seen together walking, talking, sharing coffee in one of the small outdoor cafes, or meeting after church to go down to their favorite spot on the beach. She forgot it was a small town.

Chapter 21

One evening Mrs. Wantanabe, the elderly Japanese lady who owned the fabric store, had a toothache and left early to see the dentist, asking Jana to close and lock up. She had just stepped outside and was turning the key in the lock of the door, when she heard a familiar voice call her name.

"Jana."

She turned. "Bayard! My goodness, you startled me! I didn't know you were back. I thought —"

He sauntered toward her, a cynical smile lifting the corners of his mouth under a new, neatly trimmed mustache. "I'm a fugitive." He held both hands up in a surrendering gesture. "Escaped."

"Escaped? From what?"

"A fate worse than death," he said sarcastically. "Had to save my sanity. I had no idea it took so much planning to arrange a wedding. Edith's seemed simple enough."

"That's because you didn't do anything!

You should have seen all the hard work Meipala and your Aunt Ruthie did behind the scenes. Even so, Edith rushed things so that she and Greg could go to Europe. I think his passage was already booked when they decided to get married before he went —"

"I think it was *Edith* who decided. That poor fellow didn't know what hit him."

"That's a fine way for her brother to talk," Jana chided him as she pocketed the store key and began to walk along the wooden sidewalk. Bayard fell in step alongside her. "And you certainly don't sound like a man planning to embark on the sea of matrimony himself."

Bayard didn't respond to her teasing bait. Instead, he plunged his hands into his jacket pocket and, head down, remained quiet for a few minutes.

"Do you have to go right home? Could we go somewhere and talk, Jana?" he asked her.

Surprised, she looked at him.

"Please. I really need someone — need to talk to you." He sounded serious.

"All right. We can take the beach road — that's a little longer. But if I'm not home at the usual time, Mama will wonder."

They strolled to the end of the street, then turned to take the narrower road that led to the beach.

"I must tell you, I've gained a great deal of information since I last saw you. About weddings. Things I never heard of before. Did you know that it takes six months to have a silver service monogrammed? Or that you have to order a full set of dinnerware from England a year ahead of time? Linens from France take almost as long. Did you know you cannot possibly get married without any of these?" His tone was sarcastic, with a tinge of bitterness.

Jana glanced at him. Bayard looked angry as he continued, saying, "And then there are endless parties, dinners one has to sit through, long lines of relatives to be introduced to, be ogled by, approved or disapproved by —"

"Surely Vinnie must know how you feel and can help you get out of some of these?"

"*Vinnie?* She adores all this. Revels in it. *She's* the one who's insisting on the whole shebang. I suggested eloping, even coming here to be married at the ranch —" He shook his head vigorously. "But oh no, not my darling fiancée. Besides, she has *always* spent the summer in Newport. She couldn't *dream* of being anywhere else. And of course, we will *have* to spend at least four months of every year on the mainland, besides a month in Italy."

Jana stopped walking and stared at Bayard, who also halted.

"Bayard, you don't sound very happy."

"*Happy?* Of course I'm not happy. I'm miserable. And furious. And I could kick myself every time I think of the mess I've got myself into."

Jana hardly knew what to say. At last she managed, "Does Vinnie know?"

"No, of course not. I was too much of a coward to tell her. I felt as if I were strangling. Trapped. All I told her was that I had to get back to Hawaii, to the ranch. I made some excuse about Father's needing me. It wasn't the truth, but —" He shrugged.

"I'm sorry," Jana said lamely.

Bayard turned toward her. It was fast getting dark, and his features were indistinct, but she could tell his expression was anguished.

"It was a mistake, Jana. An impulsive proposal. Blame it on too much champagne, the desire of the moment, the crazy feeling that making a decision about my future here on the island would somehow make things . . . right. But I was wrong. A girl like Vinnie doesn't any more belong *here* than I belong in Newport."

He put his hands on Jana's shoulders and, clamping his fingers tightly, drew her close so that their faces were inches apart.

"I've made a terrible mistake. It's *you* I should have proposed to. You and I, we belong here on the island, both of us. You understand. We could have —" It sounded like a groan. "I wish I'd had the good sense to ask you when I was home last year —" He broke off and pulled Jana to him. Before she could pull away or protest, he had drawn her into an embrace and was kissing her.

She was too astonished to resist. There was a desperateness in the kiss. It was neither tender, gentle, nor loving. Finally she found the strength to press both hands against his chest and break away. Breathlessly she said, "You shouldn't have done that, Bayard."

"I'm not sorry, Jana. All the way home, back here to the island, I've thought about you. What a fool I was not to recognize what we had last spring, what we could have — marry me, Jana. You won't regret it. Whatever you want, we'll do. But the island will be our home, our anchor. You love it as much as I do, but I want you to see the world. And I can take you there. And we can always come back to Hawaii, to home."

Jana listened with more understanding than she would have thought possible. What Bayard was saying echoed in her own heart.

She knew the longing, the loneliness, he must have experienced on the mainland. She felt sorry for him. But that was all. You don't give your life as a gift to someone else — not for what it can bring you, nor for sympathy, not even for love. Your life is God's gift to *you*. To use for his purpose, not someone else's.

"I'm sorry, Bayard."

"What do you mean, sorry? Don't you care for me? Can't you see the possibilities of a future with me?"

"I do care for you, Bayard, but I don't love you. Not like you seem to want me to. I'm sorry you feel you've made a mistake. But mistakes can be corrected. It would be far worse for you to go on with Vinnie if you feel it's wrong for both of you."

"Didn't you hear anything I said, Jana? It's *you* I want, *you* I need."

"I'm sorry, Bayard," she said again. "There's someone else."

His shoulders sagged. "It's Kimo, then, isn't it?"

Strangely enough, as Bayard said the words Jana knew it was true. The name she had hidden in her heart for so long came singingly to the surface. Yes, yes, she *did* love Kimo.

"Well then, I wish you the best," Bayard

sighed. "I don't think it will be easy for you or him. People will make it difficult."

They had reached the fork in the road. One side led down to the Rutherfords' house, the other up to another part of town.

"What are you going to do, Bayard?" Jana asked quietly.

"My duty, I guess. Whatever that means." He glanced at her. "It's too late to back out, I suppose. That seems to be the story. Too late. If I'd spoken earlier — before Kimo came back from Germany — would there have been a chance for me . . . for us?"

Jana hesitated. Hadn't there been a time when what Bayard could offer her had some appeal?

"I'm not sure. Maybe. But now I know for sure that whatever I felt for you, it's not what I feel for Kimo."

"I wish I could wait for that kind of certainty."

"It's worth it. But then you would hurt a lot of people —" She wished she could say something more comforting. However, she had always been taught to speak the truth with love. Was it right for Vinnie Albright — regardless of the monogrammed silver, the English china, the French linens — to marry a man who didn't love her? "I wish I could say something to help, Bayard."

"Thanks anyway, Jana." He took a few steps away from her, then half turned and raised his arm in a farewell gesture. "Aloha!"

"Aloha, Bayard," she said gently. Then he started walking fast up the road and around the bend, disappearing from her sight.

Slowly she walked home alone. In her own heart, there was a joyousness. She had acknowledged her love for Kimo, and it spread a warmth all through her that simply blotted out Bayard's warning. A warning that she would remember later.

One evening Kimo met her after work. As she was leaving the store, she saw him coming toward her. Her heart lifted like it did once when she had tried surfing and a wave caught her at its crest, creating a soaring sensation, propelling her in a rush to shore.

Kimo seemed excited. His smile was broad, his eyes sparkling. "Wait till you hear what's happened, Koana!" he greeted her. "We have got the most wonderful order. A whole dining room set — table, six chairs, a sideboard — for a house newly built in Hilo! The owner had seen some of our furniture and admired it. It was *my* design, Koana. Isn't that wonderful? This is a prominent man. He'll be doing a great deal of entertaining. Others will see our work — it may mean we are really on our way."

"Oh Kimo, I'm so proud of you! Of course, I *knew* you would succeed. Your ideas are original, your work very beautiful."

"I feel like celebrating!" he laughed, throwing his head back. "But it's not just *this* order, Koana. This means I can make a good living. It makes everything possible."

He took her arm and they started walking. Almost without thinking, they took the path past the school yard, their old way down to the beach.

"Of course, it will mean lots of hard work, long hours," he continued. "I'll probably have to stay over in Hilo to finish the set in time. He wants it when he moves into his new house. But it will be worth it. He is very influential, has wealthy friends. It may be the beginning of our becoming well known and successful."

They had reached the beach by this time. It was the most beautiful time of the day, Jana thought, her favorite time. The ocean was a pale silver, gentle waves rolled onto the sand in glistening scallops of foam, and a peaceful quiet seemed to settle over everything.

"This is just as I dreamed so many times when I was in Germany," Kimo said softly.

"Watching a sunset here on the beach — with you, Koana." He took her hand and held it.

Her heart began to pound heavily.

"This is what I've wanted to tell you for so long, Koana. All my life, maybe. Or at least since I came back from Honolulu after being away that first year. I love you. You are my dearest friend. More than a friend. More than a sister. More than that. Do you know that?"

"I think so. At least, I've hoped that. I love you, too, Kimo."

He put his arm around her shoulder and drew her close and kissed her. They watched the sun sink slowly until it was swallowed into the water, leaving the sky streaked with pink, orange. Arms around each other, they walked back up the path to the Rutherfords' house. At the gate they kissed each other again. Jana walked into the house as if in a dream. All that she had ever wanted seemed to be coming true. She could hardly believe it. It was too precious, too sweet, to share yet with anyone else. Hugging her secret close, she simply drifted back to her bedroom. There she knelt by her window, looking out into the night now studded with early stars. "Thank you, God," was all she could whisper, "for bringing my love to me."

Chapter 22

Most of the time Jana was happy, so distracted by her romance that she had almost forgotten about her quilt design, the possibility that it might win her a scholarship to art school.

So it came as startling news when she arrived home from work one evening and found her father and mother both standing out on the porch, her father waving an envelope as she came near.

"It's come, Jana. A letter from the scholarship committee! Hurry and open it. We can't wait to hear if it's what we've all hoped for you."

Jana hurried up the porch steps and, with both parents looking over her shoulder, tore open the letter. Inside was the news she had been waiting to hear for so long. A full scholarship!

But instead of being elated, a wave of shock and dismay swept over her. This meant there was no obstacle to her going to the mainland. She would be able to study at the art institute for a full year at no expense to her parents. She could follow her dream. It was coming true.

"Oh darling, we're so proud of you!" her mother said, hugging her. "You've been so good and patient, and now your talent is being rewarded."

Jana felt completely stunned, frozen by this news, while the excitement swirled all around her. Her parents' voices, interrupting each other, went in and out of her ears without Jana really hearing what they were saying. Nathan, who didn't fully understand what all the fuss was about, was skipping around the trio, blowing on his tin toy horn to add to the confusion.

Underneath it all, slowly the realization of what it meant to receive the scholarship came crushing down on Jana. This meant she would leave the island, leave Kimo. It was then she knew without doubt that she loved Kimo — and scholarship or no scholarship, she didn't want to leave him.

Jana moved through that night's impromptu celebration in a blur of mixed emotion. Her mind whirled. How could she tell her parents that she didn't want to accept the scholarship? How could she tell them, unless she and Kimo revealed their love, their hopes for a future together?

Things were happening faster than she had expected. She must talk to Kimo first.

It wasn't until late the next afternoon, when Kimo arrived from Hilo, that she had a chance to tell him. She met him at the gate, before he could go into the house and have one of her parents give him the news.

They walked down to where the beach curved in a long crescent, a row of bending palms swaying toward the glistening sand washed by lazy swirls of foam-edged surf. The cry of wheeling seabirds, the roar of the surf, merged with their thundering hearts. It was always thus when they were together after days apart.

When they reached their favorite spot, she turned toward him. He took her face in both hands, looked down into her eyes. "Koana," he murmured before he kissed her upturned mouth.

"Oh Kimo, I have something to tell you," she began haltingly.

"What is it? You look . . . sad, worried." His dark brows came together over his concerned eyes. "Tell me," he whispered, stroking back her hair, loosening the hairpins that fell silently onto the sand as her hair came uncoiled. He listened as her words tumbled out.

". . . but now it's impossible. Even though Mama and Papa think I'm happy about it, I can't go, not now. I can't accept it."

Kimo's expression became serious, and then he said slowly, "Of course you must take it. It's an opportunity you can't turn down. It's like my opportunity to go to Germany. At first I didn't want to go, didn't want to leave family, the island, *you*. But I knew I had to go, so I went — and I'm glad I did. It was the chance of a lifetime, and I couldn't afford to pass it up. None of what's happened would have happened for me if I hadn't gone." He paused. "It's the same for you, Jana. You'll have to take it. Your parents would be terribly disappointed if you didn't, and later on you'd be sorry."

She shook her head. "No, I don't think so, Kimo. I wouldn't be sorry. When I think what it means. Gone — a whole year! I couldn't afford to come home. Twelve months away from my family, everything — *you!* What about us if I go?" Jana looked at him, bewildered. She had expected him to say she couldn't go. "I don't care about the scholarship. Let someone else have it. I mean, once I thought I wanted to learn to paint really well, be an artist, but not anymore. Not since —"

"I want you to go, Jana," he said quietly.

Her eyes suddenly filled with tears. "How can you say that? I'd be miserable if I went away now, left you. I love you, Kimo."

"*Makamae,* my darling. And I love you, Jana." He hesitated, then said, "I wasn't going to ask you until — well, until I was in a better position to do it, but . . ." His voice deepened. "I want to marry you."

"Oh Kimo, I hoped you'd say that! That's what I want, too. I don't want to go away. I won't."

"Your parents may blame me if you don't, and it will hurt them, Jana. They have such high expectations for you. What would they say if we went to them and said that instead of you accepting this wonderful chance, you want to get married. To marry *me?*"

"I believe they'd understand. You should hear *their* love story. Everyone was against them marrying — sometime I'll tell you about it. But they overcame all the odds, and they *eloped* when the families opposed it. Surely they *should* understand that when two people love each other —"

"I hadn't thought we could marry for at least a year, Jana, when the business is thriving. Right now the three of us divide what comes in, put it back into the shop, for tools, lumber, whatever. If we marry now, there wouldn't be much to live on."

"What do we need? A little house, a garden? We'd be together. It would be heaven, Kimo." She touched his cheek with her hand. He caught it and kissed her palm.

Looking at her with soft, loving eyes, he said gently, "It's too much to ask. One day, I know, the business will be good — but it takes time. If we wait, we can have a wonderful life. I will build us a beautiful house, on a hilltop, overlooking the ocean. . . ."

"I don't want to wait, Kimo. It might take years. I want to work with you for the future — that would be so much better!"

Again Kimo's handsome face looked sorrowful, his dark eyes even darker, as he shook his head. "I don't think so, Jana. I'm sure your parents won't think so."

"Let me handle it, Kimo. I'll try to explain how we feel, what we want. They love me and will want me to be happy."

Impulsively she threw her arms around his neck, pulled his head down close to her cheek, let her fingers tangle in his silky dark hair.

"Oh Kimo, I love you so much. We will be so happy. Just wait and see. Everything will work out."

When Jana came into the house, her mother was in the kitchen. Jana stood in the doorway for a few minutes, trying to gather her thoughts together. She felt she might burst if she didn't tell her mother right away.

"Oh Mama, something wonderful has happened," she said.

Mrs. Rutherford raised her head, looked at her daughter. Jana's face glowed with happiness, her lips parted in a radiant smile. Some intuition chilled her mother's heart. One of the most endearing things about her daughter had always been her transparency, her openness, the truth that shone out of her eyes.

Her mother's hand, holding a knife, poised over the pineapple she was slicing. "What is it, Johanna?"

Jana should have been alerted. Her mother rarely used her christened name. But her own excitement was too high to pay attention to the serious tone of her mother's voice, the edge of caution in it. She went blithely on, saying, "Mama, Kimo has asked me to marry him, and of course I said I would. I can't go to the mainland now, Mama. We want to be married right away, or as soon as possible. Of course, he plans to speak to Papa and to you also, but isn't it a miracle? I've loved him for so long and never was sure — although I had hoped. But I always thought he'd fall in love with one of the beautiful Hawaiian girls — not someone like me. Oh, I'm so happy, Mama." Jana twirled around a couple of times, over to the table, where her mother remained silent.

Something in her mother's face halted Jana.

"What is it, Mama? What's wrong?"

Slowly Mrs. Rutherford put down her knife and wiped her hands on her apron, shaking her head.

"Oh Jana, dear child. It cannot be. It's out of the question."

"What do you mean, out of the question? I don't understand."

"Isn't it obvious that it would be impossible? It would never be accepted. What would the Kipolas think? Don't you see that?"

"No, of course not. The Kipolas love me. Tutu thinks of me just like she does Akela and Kimo. I don't know what you mean."

"Then you're deliberately trying not to, Jana. You and Kimo and Akela grew up together, of course — you were childhood friends. But marriage. That's an entirely different thing. We and the Kipolas are from different cultures, different backgrounds. . . ."

"Mama, I can't believe you're saying this."

"The Kipolas are pure Hawaiians and proud of it. They don't want the members of their family marrying out of their nationality. That's why I say it's out of the question. Neither Kimo's family nor our family would agree to such a marriage."

Stunned, Jana stared at her mother.

Her mother tried to speak more calmly, less emotionally. "I know you are very fond of Kimo, that it's more than mere friendship, but that's what I'm trying to explain. Friendship is all that it can ever be."

"No! I love Kimo. Really love him. And he loves me. Why can't you be happy for us?"

"Because I know, I can see down the road, Jana. Life has taught me about the world, about mixed relationships. *I* see what *you*, blinded by infatuation, cannot see. . . ."

"It's not infatuation," Jana said stubbornly. "I can tell the difference. I know what love is, and what I feel for Kimo *is* love."

"Darling, you're going to the mainland — you'll have all sorts of new experiences, meet new people."

"I don't want to go now! I want to stay here and marry Kimo. That's all I want."

"You're still very young, Jana."

"I'm old enough to know what I want."

Her mother's tone was very patient.

"Surely you can't mean you want to give up your scholarship? Your chance to go to art school? It's what you've wanted, what you've worked so hard for. . . ."

"None of that matters. Not if I have to leave the island, leave Kimo."

"Jana, dear." Her mother came around the table and reached out her hand to touch Jana's arm, but she jerked away.

"I don't understand, Mama. You've always liked Kimo. You've always said how considerate he was, how intelligent. . . . Why wouldn't you want me to marry him?"

Mrs. Rutherford sighed. "If you can't understand that, Jana, I don't know how else to explain it."

"I thought *you,* of all people, would understand, be glad for me, Mama. How many times have you told me about *your* mother marrying your father? How opposed her family was to the marriage, how they sent her away to forget him. Still they held out and finally got married. And you and Papa, too! Your family didn't want you to marry *him,* because he fought on the other side in the War between the States. But it didn't work. *You* eloped!" she said triumphantly. "Making me go to the mainland won't work either."

Her mother was silent for a minute, then

she turned away, went back to the table, picked up the knife. "I think we should wait to discuss this until your father comes home, after supper." She began slicing the pineapple again, saying, "Now, if you'll please set the table."

They heard Nathan's voice calling to one of his friends as he came inside, letting the screen door bang behind him.

"All right, Mama. But discussing it with Papa isn't going to change my mind. Don't think that it will."

"Until you're twenty-one, Jana, you are under obedience to your parents, remember that," her mother said coldly. Then she turned to greet Nathan, who came running into the kitchen.

Jana was too upset to eat. Feeling her mother's anxious eyes upon her, she stirred the soup, took a few spoonfuls, nibbled at a rice cake, ate part of a sliced mango. Her father, oblivious to the strain between mother and daughter, talked cheerfully about his day.

Jana glanced at him once or twice, thinking how kind he had always been, always interested in her activities, encouraging her talents. Would he turn against her now, side with her mother, agree that marriage to Kimo was impossible? She twisted her napkin nervously in her lap.

Finally the meal was over. Mrs. Rutherford rose from the table and said, "Wes, Jana has something to tell you. She has already told me — however, it is something we must all discuss together. As soon as I put Nathan to bed, I'll be back."

When her mother left, her father turned to Jana, his eyes filled with some amusement. "Well, Jana, what's this all about?"

She knew he had no idea of the seriousness of what she had to tell. She drew a long breath and poured out her heart. He listened attentively. "Kimo will come and talk to you himself, tell you his plans, ask your permission. He is doing so well, Papa. His cabinet shop is thriving — they have several big orders. He will be able to support a wife, and I plan to keep on working at the store for a while, and —"

"What about your own plans, my dear, your dreams? Your scholarship? Surely you don't imagine to marry and then take off for a year on the mainland? Have you considered all these things before you make such a statement? Marriage is not to be entered into hastily, you know, but with much prayer, much thinking."

Her mother had reentered the room and

took her place at the other end of the table. Jana looked from one to the other and then, near tears, said shakily, "I love Kimo, he loves me, and that's all that matters."

"No, my dear, that is not all that matters," her father said quietly.

Silence fell upon the room. Then her father continued, saying, "You are too young to make such a serious decision. To give up your scholarship would be foolhardy, something you would regret bitterly later. As your parents, we cannot allow you to make this mistake. You will go on with everything as planned, Jana. Your passage is booked, your living in Oakland arranged, and the school is expecting you to start with the next term." He paused. "As for marriage to Kimo, I believe you when you say you love each other. From what I know of Kimo, he is a fine, intelligent young man of character and integrity. I am sure he will agree with our decision." He paused again. "True love waits. If your love is such as you declare it to be, time apart will not weaken it — it may strengthen it. There is plenty of time to speak about marriage."

Jana pushed back her chair and stood up, her hands clenched, her breath short from trying to suppress sobs of grief and frustration. "I have to do what you say, Papa,

Mama. But I don't understand. I think there's some reason you're objecting to our getting married. But I don't think I want to hear what it is!"

Jana walked across the room and yanked open the door, letting it shut behind her just short of slamming it.

Chapter 23

When Jana awoke, sunshine was streaming in through the window. The palm fronds of the tree just outside her bedroom shadowed her quilt with its own intricate patterns. It was as if the Hawaiian design were superimposed on the coverlet her mother had made. Mrs. Rutherford's quilts always reflected her North Carolina memories. The colors were the magentas and mauves of rhododendron and the pink and tangerines of mountain laurel. The colors of Hawaiian quilts were rich and vivid, the designs bolder, just like the landscape, rich and lush.

She knew she would be expected to appear for breakfast, for family morning prayers. She had gone to bed in such misery, she didn't know how she could face her parents, pretend everything was fine when everything seemed so wrong. For a few minutes she lay huddled there, unwilling to get up. She knew that the resentment she was feeling was not right. No two people could be more loving and compassionate than her parents. They just didn't understand. How could she convince them?

Finally she threw back the covers and got up. Stretching, she padded over to the window and looked out. Warm, sweet air was blowing in. The cloudless sky met the line of the ocean like a paintbrush stroke of three different shades of blue. How could a day be so beautiful when her heart was breaking? It should be enough just to be alive. Yet Jana felt weighted by her own sadness.

As she stood there, she saw a mother and a little boy on the beach below, walking along the water's edge. The child ran ahead, dodging the frothy waves, then turned and ran back to his mother, gesturing, stopping every once in a while to look for shells. Jana's heart was suddenly wrenched. She remembered when long ago she had strolled with her mother along that same stretch of sand. They had been so close, mother and daughter. It hurt her that now this misunderstanding had come between them. Could they ever get back that old closeness? Did love always have to cause pain to someone?

Didn't her parents know that Hawaii was her home? She loved this little town, with its small, New England–style houses and their gingerbread porches and peaked roofs. Here she had grown up in view of Mauna Kea. Here the wind blew cool with the combined smell of the briny sea, the flowers, the orchards, the sugarcane fields, the coffee and orchid farms. The thought of going away was like a knife cutting deep.

And leaving Kimo. For a minute Jana closed her eyes, bringing his face into her mind — the dark eyes, so dense that sometimes they seemed impenetrable, then the smile that softened his expression and warmed her heart. . . . Long before they had declared their love, she had copied a quotation from the writings of Alphonse de Lamartine: "There is a name hidden in the shadow of my soul where I read it night and day and no other eyes have seen it." *Kimo* was that name for her.

Knowing now that he loved her too, made leaving Kimo seem impossible. "True love waits," her father had said. Was her father right? Fragments of a melody, words of a half-forgotten song, floated into her head. It was a famous Hawaiian love song: *Ke kali nei au,* "I am waiting," *Ko'u aloha.* She spoke the words softly to herself. Would it be possible to do? For a whole year?

Jana sighed. She dressed and left her

room. The house felt strangely quiet. Empty. When she went out to the kitchen, she realized why. Her mother had left a note propped against the sugar bowl on the table.

I've gone to the missionary society meeting. Took Nathan to the Caldwells'. Be back about noon.

Love Mama.

She glanced at the clock. It was after nine-thirty. But it was Saturday, and she didn't have to go to work today. She must have been worn out from crying and had slept heavily toward dawn. She poured herself some coffee from the pot still hot at the back of the stove, then wandered out on the porch to drink it.

There was so much to think about. Kimo would be coming from Hilo for the weekend, expecting to go to her father, ask for her hand. She would have to intercept him. She would have to explain what she could about her parents' opposition. She didn't want him to be hurt, to misunderstand.

She was convinced, though, that they were wrong — especially her mother, who'd explained about them being from different worlds. She and Kimo were more alike than any two people she knew. They were both

Hawaiians. They had been born on the islands, had grown up together. More than that, their spirits, their souls, were in perfect harmony. Their love was deep and real. It would endure, no matter what. Of that Jana was sure.

She finished her coffee and went back inside. Coming down the hallway, she paused outside the open door of her parents' bedroom. Her attention was drawn to the quilt covering their bed. She had seen it a thousand times, had heard the story of its making. Now it seemed to hold some kind of message for her.

Jana walked slowly into the room and over to the bed, with its tall, carved posts. She stood at its foot, looking down at the neatly sewn quilt squares.

This was the "waiting" quilt her mother had worked on for all the long, dreadful years of the war that had divided the States, when her parents lived on the mainland. Her mother had created the design to disguise the "pledge" she and Wesley Rutherford had secretly made before he left to join the Union Army. Jana now realized that this was like the *huna* Tutu had explained to her, the hidden poetic meaning to a Hawaiian quilt's design, known only to the quilter herself.

With her forefinger, Jana traced the outline of the doves in each corner of every square, the clasped hands in the center holding the tiny heart. The quilt was larger than most, because her mother, JoBeth Davison, had kept adding to it for three long years. She had pledged to keep making it until the war was over and the two lovers were reunited.

No wonder her father could say that true love waits. He and her mother were living proof that love can last through every kind of trial, tribulation, separation.

But that had been wartime, and her mother's relatives had been vigorously opposed to the match, declaring Wes a traitor to his people for siding with the Union against the Southern Confederacy.

For her and Kimo it was different. Jana did not really understand why her parents seemed so much against their love, their wanting to marry. She thought of her father's words again. She was willing to wait if in the end she and Kimo could marry.

Why were her parents so concerned, so reluctant to give their consent, even their blessing, to a future marriage? She did not know how to prove to her parents that their love was true. Her plans were as vague and unformed as the drifting clouds overhead.

But somehow she knew she would find a way.

She knew she needed assurance, help. Instinctively she went down on her knees, put her head into folded hands, and whispered, "Dear God, tell us what to do and we will do it. I want to be in Your will. I know that's all that matters. Please help us."

Jana had been taught that asking for a sign from God was not something to do lightly. However, having also been taught that parents were His earthly representatives and were to be obeyed, Jana prayed to accept their decision. But she wanted to feel that it really *was* God's will for her.

The next day, she had her Sunday school class to teach but was distracted by her own turbulent mind. It probably didn't help when she went in to face fifteen restless, active, mischievous five- and six-year-olds. Singing always seemed to give them a chance to vent their energy, so she had them all join hands and form a circle and sing some of the hymns she had taught them. "Jesus Loves Me" was one everyone loved and knew the words to and sang at the top of their lungs. Round and round the little group went, singing it over and over. Then one little girl piped up with the first line of another hymn. Raising her voice above the rest, she sang, "Jesus loves the little children, all the children of the world. Red and yellow, black and white, they are precious in his sight. Jesus loves the little children of the world." All of a sudden, Jana's heart was struck as she looked around the circle at all the little faces, all the little mouths open, their voices singing with complete assurance that they were loved and accepted by the Creator of the universe. She was hard put not to start crying. She gazed at each child. Of course it was true. Hawaiian, Chinese, Portuguese, Japanese, or a mixture — they were all God's beloved children.

When the older girls came over to take the smaller children out to play in the churchyard during the service for the adults, Jana, deep in thought, walked over to the church. She slipped into one of the back pews. The choir was just filing out, and Reverend Homakaa was stepping up to the pulpit.

She had asked for a sign but had not expected to get such a clear one. She heard the minister's voice say, "I am taking my sermon today from Acts 10:34–35, where Peter states, 'God is no respecter of persons. In every nation he whoever fears him and works righteousness is accepted by him.' In both Galatians 3:28 and Colossians 3:11, that same theme is repeated: 'In Christ there is neither Greek nor Jew, slave nor free, nor male or female. All are one in Christ.' "

To be truthful, Jana did not really hear much of Reverend Homakaa's sermon. She had opened her Bible and read and reread the passages he had quoted. *Thank you, Lord,* she said in her heart. *That is what I needed to hear.*

The doxology was sung in Hawaiian: *"Ho'o-na-ni-i ka Ma-ku-a-mau,* Praise God from whom all blessings flow," and Jana rose to sing it with a grateful heart.

During the closing hymn, Jana left quietly. She needed to be alone before joining her parents and telling them she had accepted their decision.

She could still hear the voices of the congregation raised in praise as she took the path that led down to the beach.

Suddenly she saw the day in its glorious beauty, the blue sky and sea merging almost seamlessly, the whisper of music in the palm fronds tossed by the soft wind.

God must see his world like a quilt, she thought, *made up of all different textures, colors, designs, sizes, shapes, all blending into a beautiful whole.* She smiled at her own imagery and then thought that perhaps God smiled, too.

Chapter 24

A few days before Jana was scheduled to leave for Honolulu and from there take the ship to the mainland, Tutu Kipola sent for her. Jana's heart was heavy as she went up the familiar path to the small house shaded by the wide banana tree leaves, through the garden lush and brilliant with flowers.

She found Tutu sitting at her frame on the porch, busy quilting.

"Aloha, Tutu," she said, embracing her.

"Aloha, Koana," Tutu replied, using her Hawaiian name. "Come sit down here beside me and tell me — are you all ready to go?"

Jana tucked her skirt up and sat down on a low stool at the side of Tutu's chair. "Yes, everything is packed," she sighed, then impulsively burst out, "You know I don't want to go. I'm just doing it for my parents' sake."

Tutu took a few tiny stitches more before raising her head and meeting Jana's soulful eyes.

"Respect for your parents is not a thing to be sorry for, Koana. You would regret it if you went against their wishes."

"I hate leaving. I'll miss . . . *everything* so much. It will all be so different."

"Yes, that's true, Koana. It will be different, but you will learn many new things, many new ways."

"I'm happy here. I don't care about new things." Jana hesitated, then rushed on, saying, "Oh Tutu, the *real* reason, the *main* reason, I don't want to leave is Kimo. You know we love each other. What I really want to do is stay here, be with him. I'm afraid —" She caught herself before finishing the sentence.

"Afraid, Koana? Of what are you afraid?"

"Of losing" — Jana thrust out her hands in a sweeping gesture — "this, all this. And maybe . . . of losing Kimo."

"But what you carry in the heart is never lost, little one," Tutu said gently. "If your love is real, true, it will last. Separation will not destroy love. It may even make it stronger."

"Please don't tell me that true love waits, Tutu. That's what my father says — that's why I'm going. He thinks this is some kind of test for Kimo and me."

"And maybe he is right."

"We've already been tested. First when Kimo went to the academy on Oahu, then all the time he was in Germany. My parents simply don't understand. They think we are too different, that we would not be happy, but they're wrong. We were children together — all my memories of my childhood include him. Kimo was the most wonderful playmate, full of fun and imagination, always ready to laugh and enjoy whatever the moment held. Even as a boy, he was sensitive to and tender toward animals, had an appreciation for the natural things — the shells, the tiny creatures in the tide pools, even the *gheckos,* the little lizards that are everywhere, the ones most people dislike."

Tutu laughed and nodded her head.

Warming to her subject, Jana went on, saying, "When he came back from Germany and I saw him again, every other man I had ever met simply faded into the background. Everyone else seemed smaller, paler, by comparison. Now that we're grown up, I know so much more about him, so many things that I admire and love. It's breaking my heart to leave."

Tutu put aside her needle and thread, carefully folded the quilt she was working on, got to her feet, and said, "Come inside, I want to show you something."

Jana followed her into the cool interior of the cottage. Tutu went to the large closet and opened its doors and pulled out one of the sliding drawers. Jana knew this was where Tutu kept her treasury of quilts, alternating them on her own beds or keeping them for when opportunities arose to give them as gifts. Now she carefully lifted one out, slowly unrolling it so that Jana could see it at full length.

It was exquisite. Pink and green on a paler green background, the elaborate scrolls around the scalloped edge surrounding interwoven wreaths of flowers, the circling design repeating itself, forming a medallion in the center.

Jana drew in her breath. "It's beautiful, Tutu," she whispered.

"It's for you. I made it for you. To take with you now so that every time you see it, use it, you will be reminded of the island and what the message of this quilt is. . . ."

Jana waited for Tutu to tell her what the secret of the design was, although longed to ask.

"I call it *Ka Makani, Ka'ili Aloaha,* Wind That Wafts Love from One to Another. The encircling wreaths, with flowers you recognize by their shapes as being island flowers — plumeria, hibiscus — represent two winds that blow, meeting each other, wafting in opposite directions, then coming back together to meet in a perfect circle. You and Kimo are like that: one calm, steady; the other adventurous, going hither and thither; both unsure, then blending in one harmonious center. See? Understand?"

Jana nodded. "Yes, I think I do. We both have to find that center, even as we search in different directions?"

Tutu smiled and the radiance that was in her shone in her eyes and smile, making her brown, wrinkled face almost beautiful.

"Oh Tutu, mahalo from the bottom of my heart! How can I ever thank you enough?"

Tears came and streamed unabashedly down Jana's cheeks as she hugged Tutu.

Later as she carried the quilt, which was swathed in protective tissue paper, back along the road home, Jana's heart was full of tenderness. She knew that every stitch of the quilt had been an act of love. She had never appreciated Tutu's caring and wisdom as much. In the space of the afternoon, she had eased Jana's heartache, made her more fully understand that life sometimes requires sacrifice, effort, and time to make something beautiful of it, just as much as is required in the making of a quilt.

Jana knew she would cherish Tutu's gift

all the time she was away, daily learning the lessons it taught. Then one day she would bring it back to the island — one day it would have a place of honor in the home Jana was sure she would share with Kimo.

When she got home, she did not show the quilt to her mother. She was afraid, somehow, that it might hurt her. After all, her mother had also made two quilts for Jana to take with her.

Her mother's quilts were beautiful. But they spoke of *her* home, her land — of the mountain laurel and pines of North Carolina, of the golden poppies and purple lupine of California, where she had lived before she came to Hawaii. It was Tutu's quilts that spoke to Jana's heart.

Carefully putting Tutu's quilt at the bottom of her trunk, Jana said to herself, *On the surface, I am doing what my parents want me to do, but I am my own person. My destiny is my own. They will always be haoles, not of this island. I was born here, belong here — this is my heart's home, to which I shall always return.*

The evening before she was to leave for Honolulu, Jana went in to say a private good-bye to her father, since he would not be there to see her off. She knocked softly at his study door, waited for his answer before turning the knob and entering.

He was at his desk, a pile of school reports spread out on its surface. He turned toward her, smiling. "Come in, my dear," he greeted her, holding out one hand. "Come, sit down," he invited. "Well, Jana, so it's tomorrow then and you're off — into the great world, is it? It's all come soon, so much sooner than I —" He broke off. Still holding her hand, he drew her closer. "Sit down, let me have a good, long look at you." She sat and her throat tightened as her father's tender gaze lingered upon her. "You're very talented, Jana, and I hope you realize it is a gift that you should cherish and develop — I think you will. I feel confident that although we may not have been able to prepare you for all you're going to be facing in the future, at least we have given you a foundation that will stand you in good stead, whatever happens. Your mother and I count on you, Jana, to make the most of this opportunity." He looked at her for a long moment before going on. "This is hard for you, I know, but hardships and sacrifices and separations from those you love are all part of life. They are all part of what we each have to learn."

"Yes, Papa, I know." Quite suddenly Jana saw him as through a stranger's eyes. Her beloved father looked worn, suddenly older than she remembered noticing before. Everything, now that she was leaving, seemed to have added significance. She had never given much thought to how wearing his job must be, the constant interisland traveling, staff, committees, school board, student-teacher meetings, problems, complaints. Not wanting to cry, she got up and leaned down and kissed his cheek.

"Thank you, Papa, for everything."

"We'll miss you, dear, but it's the right thing, and the time will pass more quickly than you think it will now."

"Yes, Papa," she whispered. For his sake, Jana did not let him see the tears just under the surface, the heartache she was hiding. She would spare him that.

At the door she turned and looked back. His head was already bent over the papers on his desk. Quietly she tiptoed out. Kimo was coming and this last good-bye would be the hardest.

They held hands, fingers locked, palms together, and walked down the path to the deserted evening beach. A palm tree, uprooted by a recent storm, lay on its side. Its scattered dry fronds crackled under their feet as they picked their way among large pieces of bleached driftwood until they found one to sit upon.

Kimo was unusually quiet. Jana's departure was the dark cloud that had hung over them these past weeks. They had avoided facing it until it now. Jana realized that he, more than anyone else, understood what her going away meant. He'd had the same kind of opportunity, and it had meant two years in Germany, away from Hawaii. Exile!

She knew Kimo was struggling against his own natural desire to keep her with him, so he could give her the courage she would need to say good-bye. A year, twelve long months — and then the future loomed uncertainly. The fear that lurked in both of their minds was that even then something might prevent their being together. Perhaps one of them might change — although Jana could not believe that would happen. Still, it lay heavily on both their minds, unspoken.

The clouds were turning pink, orange. For a few minutes the sky turned brilliant. Then the sun began its descent. Once, Kimo had told her that watching a sunset was to him almost a spiritual experience, so she was silent now beside him. The awe both felt was tinged with sadness. It would be a long time before they would share another sunset together.

If only, Jana thought wistfully, *it could al-*

ways be like this, never change, remain this beautiful moment, caught in an eternity. She put her head on Kimo's shoulder. His arm went around her waist, drawing her close, and his chin rested on her hair. She could smell the scent of wood, the faint fragrance of sandalwood and koa that sometimes clung to him.

Kimo began to speak to her in a low tone, in both English and Hawaiian, so that the words sounded almost like poetry.

"Someday we will build our home on the top of the bluff, overlooking the beach, where the wind blows the palm fronds, making enchanted music for only us to hear. . . ."

As Jana listened to his deep voice, melodic and soft in her ears, she was filled with happiness, knowing deep within her that this was the language of their love, the combination of two cultures, two minds, hearts, spirits, so closely joined that no translation was necessary. How many people in the world were lucky enough to have this kind of perfect understanding? In spite of her pain at parting, she was convinced that this was the person with whom she was destined to spend the rest of her life in this special place. They had pledged their love, just as her parents had, years ago, in the face of a long, dreadful separation, and it would last, whatever lay ahead.

Kimo put his fingers under her chin and turned her face toward him, then kissed her with infinite tenderness. *"Aloha, Mau loa, kau a kau,"* he said gently.

"Aloha, Kimo," she replied.

Chapter 25

May 1889

Once aboard the steamer to Honolulu, the fact that she was actually leaving Hawaii and on her way to the mainland became real to her.

Things had moved so quickly. Her father had business in Kona that morning and so had said his good-bye, giving her a new Bible as a going-away present. Then, accompanied by her mother and Nathan and surrounded by her luggage, she went by wagon to the dock, where Akela and Kimo were waiting to see her off. Of course, she and Kimo had already said their private good-bye. Now the unspoken things lay too deep to share, but they understood their mutual silence. The things they *had* spoken, the promises exchanged, they both considered as sacred as though they had been said before an altar.

At last the small boat's whistle sounded.

Eyes brimming with tears, Jana hugged Nathan, embraced her mother, and said her final alohas. Akela and Kimo both had leis for her. Akela's was of carnations and plumeria blossoms, Kimo's of yellow hibiscus. Knowing how far she was going and how long it would be before her return, it took every ounce of Jana's will to give Kimo the traditional kiss, whisper, "Aloha," turn away, and board the boat.

As the boat pulled out of the harbor, gradually her tears stopped. By the time she arrived in Honolulu, Jana had regained her composure. She realized that for the first time in her life, she was entirely on her own. Nervous but excited, she asked directions to the information office. There she was told that the ship SS *Umatilla* was already loading passengers, and she was directed to its moored place at the dock.

Clutching her ticket, heart thumping, Jana went up the gangplank. At the top she was greeted by the ship's officer, who then turned her over to a uniformed stewardess who led her through the passageway to the cabin.

"You'll be sharing it, dear. With one of the missionary wives going home on furlough. She hasn't arrived yet, so you can have your pick of bunk and chest," the woman said briskly. "When you've settled in a bit, you'll want to go back up on deck. The farewell is always interesting, band playing and all." She smiled, then leaned forward and said in a stage whisper, "You're going to have royalty for fellow passengers this trip." She gave Jana a wink and then went out the door.

Royalty? Jana thought. Who could she mean? It was all very mysterious and exciting. She would be sure to take the stewardess' advice and go back up on deck and see what was going to happen.

Jana explored the small, narrow cabin, then opened her suitcase and hung up the things she would need for the week's journey. Most of her clothes were packed in her trunk. She unpacked her toilet articles, put them away. Then she lifted out the lovely quilt Tutu had given her, from the bottom of the larger of her two suitcases. Before placing it at the foot of her narrow bunk, she smoothed its delicate design tenderly. It would always remind her of the loving acceptance Kimo's family had given her. It symbolized *ohana,* the Hawaiian word meaning family in the fullest sense of the word. Ohana, a beautiful reality. Because Kimo loved her, all the Kipolas loved her.

She shoved both suitcases under her bunk, then went out of the cabin, down the passageway, and up the steps. As she stepped out onto the deck, she noticed an audible stir among the passengers, a murmur that grew into a buzz circulating throughout the groups of people on deck. Aware that she was about to witness something unusual and exciting, Jana found a place at the railing just in time to see that it was the royal entourage coming up the gangplank. Jana could hardly believe her eyes. Princess Kaiulani!

Of course, she had often seen many pictures of the child who would one day be Hawaii's queen, but she had never dreamed she would ever see her in person. She recognized her immediately. At fourteen, the princess was exquisite with her satiny golden skin, her thick, curling black hair, her rounded nose, her sweet, vulnerable mouth. She held the promise of even greater beauty as she grew into womanhood.

The princess was accompanied by the tall, splendid-looking gentleman who was her father, the Scotsman Archibald Cleghorn, husband of the Hawaiian princess Likelike, the younger sister of King Kalakaua.

As they came on board, for a moment Jana found herself close enough to look into the small, beautiful face of the princess. There was an instant of eye contact. Their gaze locked. In that moment, Jana saw something she recognized within the velvety depths of the dark brown eyes. Something for which she felt immediate empathy. *Poor little girl! I know exactly how you feel. My heart aches, too. To leave this beloved land, to go to something strange, new, unknown. My heart aches for you.*

All around Jana another rippling murmur swirled. Following the princess and her father came a tall, lanky, spectrally thin gentleman, a *haole* whom Jana also recognized. She had seen him photographed with the king. It was the famous writer-poet, Robert Louis Stevenson! He was a good friend of the king and of the royal family and was often a guest at the palace. Hollow-cheeked, long of nose, the man nevertheless had eyes that twinkled, and his mouth, under a drooping mustache, had a humorous tilt. He seemed to enjoy the celebrity he had among the people clustered on deck.

He was escorting an elderly woman. His mother? She looked like an aristocratic Scotswoman. Her dark, austere clothing oddly contrasted with the rest of the color-fully dressed company and the lei of brilliant flowers she was wearing.

Loud whispers ran from one passenger to the other, all crowding to see what they could see yet keeping a respectful distance from the group, to whom the ship's crew were now showing decided deference.

Jana was thrilled to see, in person, the creator of some of her favorite stories. As the group passed out of view on their way to their suite of cabins, the other passengers thronged again to the railing to watch as the huge ship moved slowly out of the harbor. People leaned forward to get their last glimpse of Honolulu.

Jana felt the painful lump rise into her throat again as she looked down at the wake of cerulean blue waves taking them further out to sea. The scent of the plumerias and carnations in her leis rose fragrantly — she hated to part with them, and yet she was determined to carry out the tradition. According to the old legend, if a lei thrown from a departing ship floated out to sea, you would not return, but if it went instead toward the shore, that meant you would come back to Hawaii.

Gently she lifted the leis over her head and, one by one, tossed them over the railing as far as she could throw. Then she leaned forward, anxiously watching the direction in which they floated.

She held her breath, trying to keep her eyes on the strands of white, yellow, and lavender flowers riding on the surface of the water. First they bobbed this way and that. *Oh no!* she thought, as they seemed almost directionless. Then suddenly the yellow hibiscus lei seemed caught in a whirling wave and, like a skilled surfer, drifted *shoreward.*

The relief she felt brought tears to her eyes. The scene blurred and she blinked, trying to keep the lei in sight as it moved inland toward the beach.

Immediately the Scripture Matthew 6:21 came into her mind: "Where your treasure is, there your heart will be also."

"Yes, yes, I will come back," Jana promised herself. "Back to the land of my birth, of my heart, of my love.

"I will return. . . . *Aloha nui loa.* . . ."

How to Make a Hawaiian Quilt

In the eighteenth and nineteenth centuries, Christian missionaries first brought the basic quilt-making techniques to the Hawaiian islands, and before long, a local tradition sprang up that diverged widely from that found in the continental United States. The nature of the Hawaiian quilt makes it nearly impossible to outline a simple method of making one, but those readers who are experienced in basic quilting will be aided in making a Hawaiian quilt by observing the following principles.

First of all, Hawaiian quilts do not rely on the building up of smaller repetitive square-and-diamond patterns in the way that many traditional quilts do. Rather, they display one large, overall design that can even look at times to the uneducated eye like a folded-paper cutting of a Christmas snowflake. Usually, a floral, vine, or other decorative pattern radiates from the center of the quilt, covering the entire surface with its pattern. The pattern repeats, in a sense, like a pie cut into four, six, or eight pieces, all radiating from the center. To get a sense of the traditional designs, we recommended that you study the designs in one of the books listed below.

Second, the Hawaiian use of color is different than in other quilt traditions. White is usually used for the background color, and the main pattern, which is frequently a silhouette motif, is usually rendered in a single bold color. This gives the quilt a brightly toned and high-contrast look, which is a reflection of the sunlit islands themselves. Sometimes other colors are added with smaller decorative pieces to the main pattern if more detail is desired.

Third, unlike most American quilts, every Hawaiian quilt is quite different. A Hawaiian quilt maker varies her design from quilt to quilt, developing a distinctive and recognizable style, but seldom repeating a pattern or element. This is different from Appalachian quilts, for instance, in which common forms and patterns are widely shared among quilt makers and repeated often from community to community. In a sense, the Hawaiians have a very strong tradition of individual expression in their quilt making, which makes this form especially appealing.

Aside from these differences, the techniques largely remain the same, from the designs being cut and appliquéd onto the layered white fabric to the final stitching together. For details of the actual stitching techniques and sample designs, you might want to refer to the following books, which can be ordered from your local bookstore: Elizabeth Root, *Hawaiian Quilting* (New York: Dover, 1989); Milly Singletary, *Hawaiian Quilting Made Easy* (Singletary Publications, 1992); and Reiko M. Brandon, *The Hawaiian Quilt* (Honolulu: Honolulu Arts, 1989).